About Books by Alice Denham:

Secrets of San Miguel

"Alice Denham—writer/playmate/muse—has written a
mystical memoir about the Mexican town of San Miguel,
an artist community far from the maddening and very
mundane crowd. Alice paints a stirring portrait of the
impoverished natives, mingling, sometimes uneasily, among
the norteamericanos. Her vignettes cover a motley group,
including charming conmen, horny gringas, lazy hippies,
brutal policía and lost souls searching for...something. A
dynamic performance from a master storyteller. Prepare to be
enchanted."

> —**Dermot McEvoy**
> author of *Our Lady of Greenwich Village*
> and *Terrible Angel*

"In her latest book, *Secrets of San Miguel,* Denham reveals the
kind of insider stories that make tour guides shiver with glee
and tourists plan their next trip.
  "Borrachos in bars, stoners on cobblestones, amorous
flings in the afternoon, of course, the occasional murder,
Denham's *Secrets of San Miguel* sounds like a telenovela but
reads like classic literature. You'll love it. I sure did."

> —**Mark Saunders**
> author of *Nobody Know the Spanish I Speak*

"In *Secrets of San Miguel* you find true and touching love,
a friendly neighborhood murderer, skin-crawling evil
and extreme nuttiness in the same paragraph. An express
enthraller, a one-sitting book if there ever was one."

> —**Jim Morris**
> author of *The Devil's Secret Name,*
> Bernal Díaz del Castillo Prize for his
> Vietnam memoir, *War Story*

Sleeping WIth Bad Boys:
Literary New York in the 1950s and 1960s

Nothing less than an eyewitness account of the unfolding of
an era. Denham's personal memories of key writers segue into
keen literary criticism, while her trials as a woman author and
model are firmly set against the feminist movement of the
Sixties.

—Wim Coleman, review in *Atención*

AMO, the Feminist Centerfold from Outer Space

Denham writes better about sex than anyone.

—*Ms.* magazine

My Darling From the Lions

When Miss Denham is being lyrical, she is capable of some
really incredible language

—*Sunday New York Times Book Review*

Alice also has written for *The New York Times, Village Voice,
The Nation, Cosmopolitan, New York magazine, Playboy, The
Washingtonian, Publishers Weekly, Confrontation, Best of the
Missouri Review, Great Tales of City Dwellers, San Miguel Review,
Solamente en San Miguel,* etc. She has taught creative writing
at Yale, Smith, University of Toronto, and John Jay College of
Criminal Justice.

ALICE DENHAM
(1927–2016)
is the author of two memoirs
Sleeping With Bad Boys:
A Jucy Tell-all of Literary New York
In The 1950s-1960s
and *Secrets of San Miguel,*
and the novels *AMO* and
My Darling From The Lions.

"Wry, gossipy, apparently possessed of an
extraordinary memory and nobody's fool ...."

—Stacy D'Erasmo, *The New York Times,* 11/19/2006

She is the only *Playboy* Playmate who ever had a short story
and a centerfold feature published in the same issue of *Playboy*
magazine. Her story was made into a festival prizewinning
movie.

She is a founding member of the
National Organization for Women.

Alice's literary publications and
family papers are being preserved
in the Southern Historical Collection
at UNC Chapel Hill.

AMO

AMO

The Feminist Centerfold from Outer Space

ALICE DENHAM

CARRBORO, NC

This novel was first published in hardcover by Coward, McCann & Geoghegan in 1974, ISBN 0698106253 (ISBN13: 9780698106253). In 2010 it was re-released as an Author's Guild Press BackinPrint edition, published by IUniverse. ISBN 9781450204545. Those editions are no longer in print.

ISBN: 978-1-935178-38-5

Library of Congress Control Number: 2016911849

Drowned in Madeira wine, two flies began to recover life.
—*Benjamin Franklin*

CARRBORO, NC
WWW.MADEIRAPRESS.COM

Epilogue: Amo's Disclaimers

AMO is not ammunition.

W.R. is not Women's Rights.

D.O.D. is not Department of Defense.

Meat is not *Playboy*.

TIDBITS are not Playmates or Bunnies.

GOBBLERS are not turkeys.

G.M.C. is not General Motors Corporation.

HOUSEHUMPS
        &   abound.
DUMPTRUCKS

Does MAL mean bad or sick?

Does WHIT mean witty or witless?

MARUVIA is a condition known to women.

Maybe W.R. *is* Women's Rights.

THE GOBBLING DEFICIENCY is a male malady.

For all those who survive alone

Acknowledgments

Thanks to Arlene and Gerald Lampert for their support and to Bill Henderson and Elaine Markson for their excellent taste. And thanks to the MacDowell Colony for recognizing that art is a reality.

Any writer knows that when the image of the heroine changes, the plot changes with her.

—CATHERINE DRINKER BOWEN
"We've Never Asked a Woman Before"

The camera does not kill, so it seems to be all a bluff—like a man's fantasy of having a gun, knife, or tool between his legs. Still, there is something predatory in the act of taking a picture. To photograph people is to violate them, by seeing them as they never see themselves, by having knowledge of them they can never have. To photograph is to turn people into objects that can be symbolically possessed. To photograph someone is a sublimated murder, just as the camera is the sublimation of a gun.

We are image-junkies now. It is a glorious form of mental pollution.

—SUSAN SONTAG
"Photography"

Courage is the price that life exacts for granting peace.

—AMELIA EARHART

Prologue: Ah-mo, 196–

Amo's mother says it's pronounced Ah-mo, that she named her after the orphanage where she found the child—the (A)tlanta (M)unicipal (O)rphanage. I love, Amo means. Amo amas who? Does anyone love Amo now that she lives in New York?

In her novel, Amo claims it stands for Authorized Maruvian Operative. W.R. goes along with her on that. Amo is talking to the Wrist Radar now, griping rather.

AMO: *"I don't like to complain, but you messed up."*

W.R.: *"We have difficulty measuring in Earth millimeters."*

AMO: *"Your timing was off—and that's fatal here. You combined the wrong elements."*

W.R.: *"We tried to optimize, that's all—the sex appeal of Marilyn Monroe, the mind of Simone de Beauvoir."*

AMO: *"So that's what it's supposed to be."*

W.R.: *"It?"*

AMO: *"This ridiculous disguise. I look like cake icing."*

W.R. (huffily): "Sorry. We didn't want you to get lost in the shuffle."

AMO: "Marilyn is already passé, don't you know that? I have to do figure modeling—nude."

W.R.: "What's wrong with that?"

AMO: "I'd earn more clothed."

W.R.: "Let me see—it says here: 'AMO COOVE —Programmed to write glorious novel to be made into movie starring her, then play, then musical, then TV show, starring Amo for life run. Begin as model.' That's what it says."

AMO (laughing): "You sound like an afternoon soap opera. Why didn't you make me a black Jewish male radical—or a talk show host—or a rich girl? Everybody likes rich girls."

W.R.: "But you look great—so blonde and cuddly and cat-eyed—"

AMO: "And tiny."

W.R.: "Yum—yes."

AMO: "You think tiny is cute, W.R.?"

W.R.: "Yeeaaah."

AMO: "I'm the size of a Puerto Rican, a Vietnamese. I weigh 100 pounds."

W.R.: "So?"

AMO: "How can I defend myself? Who ever heard of a warrior that looked like that?"

W.R.: "Warrior, hm? Says here, 'Experiment in Adaptation of Superior Maruvian Being to Inferior Hostile Environment.' Is that how you feel?"

AMO (cascading laughter): "When I don't feel

angry, I feel grand! High as the sky . . . or low as a lie."

W.R.: "Wow, are you ever adapting!"

AMO: "Seriously, W.R., can't I be a movie star instead? Or even a housewife? Nobody in her right mind wants to be a novelist today."

W.R. (after a pause): ". . . Precisely, my dear."

Amo lived alone, wrote alone, knew almost no one. When she saw couples, when she saw families with children, she looked on them as marvels. She posed for photographers—one man and Amo in a silent studio—then went back to her seedy one-room. And cried. Then pulled herself together and worked on the Maruvian saga at night. It was getting harder and harder to remember Maruvia. Then in a flash she could see the coastal outline as they took off, the land masses, the ball, then purple space that grew dim and faded in her memory. A fantasy for survival.

Secretly Amo feared she had no identity. What was she—her desires, her fears, her small talents? Out the window she tugged at a star to make it fall for her. Not a sway. Not even a whimper.

Maruvia—all her ten-year-old friends had been more beautiful; after all, they were younger. Even in Atlanta, eyes on the street would swing to her best friend, the Beauty. She'd been all but invisible. Perhaps that was why she modeled now.

Chapter 1
Produce B'iness

Out of the subway, Amo headed for the grimy
storefront on Ninth Avenue in the Twenties. She
walked past it, down the block, before she could make
herself turn and plunge in. Consider yourself lucky
they'll pay to see you naked and vulnerable. Go on,
enter. A dreary bunch of men lounged about the front.
"Hi . . . hi, hello, everybody—out in a flash." Back
to the dingy cubbyhole called the Dressing Room,
where everything was too dirty to touch.

Sy leaned in and muttered, "Let 'em wait ten
minutes. I think we get a couple more fish. And I got a
private session for you after—one hour." Sy—small,
bald and smiley—thought he was a real con man with
this backroom Photo Studio operation.

"Swell." Amo hung her jeans on a hook and ripped
into a bright hanky of a bikini, sheer beach coat over
her shoulders. They never liked this much costume,
but for suspense she had to start somewhere. Amo
played tough to hide her naïveté.

"How 'bout Toosday and Toisday next week?"

"Fine."

Sy marked it carefully in the book and went out to greet a couple more live ones.

Amo combed her hair, redrew her eyes and mouth, patted powder on her nose. You have to eat, she told the rusty mirror; you're hooked on food. She'd gone around the media, shown them her *ensalada* of credentials—BA (Phi Beta Kappa), University of Texas; MA University of Salamanca; reporter on Tampa *Tribune*; TV newscaster (women's news and gambling forecast), Las Vegas; two short stories published in revered (unread) literary reviews—and they'd yawned politely, stared at her tits, and asked her to lunch. Not exactly Ivy League pedigrees there, and then she was emphatically the wrong sex.

The newspaper and magazine offices looked like factories for converting words to litter, the publishing houses like mortuaries for stuffed owls, the TV offices floated in chaos. Amo hated them all because none of them would hire her. A book publisher offered her the quaint position of secretary if she had shorthand. She didn't. Then Amo discovered her destiny: she could model four-five hours a week and make barely enough bread—and have time to write. Real time, not exhausted time. Back then, in 196–, nude modeling was wacky, outlandish, risky, and that suited Amo. Every time she flew through the air, reaching for the rungs, she knew they might not be there. But she loved to leap. At night in her dreams she glided through the galaxies, checking things out, conversing with W.R.

As she shined her nipples and cleavage with Vaseline, Amo swore she'd keep writing the Maruvian saga if it killed her. She fastened the bikini top too tight so her breasts would bulge over and look immense. Vulgar taste these creeps had, and Amo knew how to feed it. Even if she had to Sell It on the corner for a quarter! She sobbed once, then kept from blinking so the tears wouldn't smudge her elaborate eye makeup. If it got in her eyes, it burned like alcohol. Keep writing, she threatened her image, pounding the dressing table till dust flew. Anger helped.

Amo was far angrier than she knew. She hated the respectable media that wouldn't hire her, forced her into the demimonde to survive. If she'd gone to Smith or Vassar, they said. Amo, with her outlandish background, was a peon. She didn't know the Smith and Vassar girls weren't hired either, except as secretaries. Like most women back then, Amo thought it was her own fault, that she was inadequate in some undecipherable way. What on Earth would she do without W.R. and Maruvia?

Amo swept onto the set counting the house. Six so far—$18. She got $20 for the hour or $3 per head, whichever was highest. She got $20 for the private session after—a $40 day. This was her source of bread while breaking into commercial modeling. Her model agency would not have approved; neither did Amo. Amo was always having to do some Earthly thing she loathed and pretend she liked it. Her first job after her MA was as a waitress. This was briefer.

The set was a white paper roll banked by a couple of rickety lights. Beyond that stood six gents in a jumble of middle-age collapse—baggy pants, droopy guts hung with hard gleaming tubes of camera poking out front. They pay to see you cower, Amo. Don't cower—command. Make it fun, make it a lark. Tease the process and make them accept the joke.

"Hello, everybody, I'm Amo Coove"—they looked uptight and avid—"your friendly pinup girl." They relaxed a bit. "We'll start with this, then I'll get into less and less, okay?"

"Like nothing?" mouthed a toughie.

Amo held up a sweet finger, "After the build-up." Sy jiggled the lights about and Amo began to work. She did a couple of fast all-Maruvian girl poses, escalating to sheer glee. Then stood with hip pushed out, hands lifting hair, mouth agape, eyes sleepy, as if she were in some slanted corner of ecstasy, this thanks to Brigitte or Sophia or somebody.

"Amo, I can tell you love your work," one of the men said. "You're so natural."

Amo guffawed at that one. She could put it On, Off, at the drop of an eyelid. After all, she was brought up in the South, where womenfolk and blacks learn to needle Old Massah with dropkick wit, fast turns, and fleet insinuations instantly denied. Irony, some folks call it. "You're a dreadful tease, " said her mother, the Judge.

Kneeling, working at a three-quarter angle, Amo lowered the forward strap of her bikini and made her face pure tease. Better get rid of the top before they started grumbling. She unhooked the back—"About time," somebody lipped—and held the top barely covering her nipples. Silence—they shot away happily on that one. She rolled over onto a hip, her back to them, holding the top aloft like a trophy. Then rolled forward for their first bare breast shot. Cameras clicked like crazy for the next twenty minutes as she swirled from pose to pose, combining ballet and gymnastics with raving tits and rhapsodic Marilyn smiles, big enough to swallow a boa constrictor. When she was into it, she could sway the men like a faith healer. Finally she even turned herself on, this freeze-frame dancer.

Whisked off, returned with only a plaid scarf tied around her hips, big bow almost covering her frilly box. "My hula skirt," she laughed. Back then pubic hair was completely illegal and Amo went to such lengths to cover hers that she was sometimes startled to discover it was still there.

At the back of the room lounged a large blue fuzz, young and smiling.

"Hi," Amo said, surprised.

"Hi," the cop smiled back. The men ignored him.

Amo posed with her hands in front of her breasts, as if she were trying to hide the stiff nipples, actually revealing them; they loved coy stuff. A mashed-face guy with a cigar snuck around to the side where he could see more. "To the front, please." She covered herself, for the cop's benefit as well as her own. He chomped down on the cigar, gave her a disgusted leer; she gave him a haughty eye and he shuffled back into place.

"Okay, time," called Sy. "That's all, fellas."

"Hey, she's really great," someone said.

"Well, that's Amo Coove."

"When you on next, Amo?"

"Next Tuesday. Unless you want a private session." Amo, selling.

"You're too rich for me, baby."

They went out jolly, cop too.

Amo Coove was one of the first respectable nudes. Nobody with a college degree had ever been seen with her clothes off. It was a good time to pose nude, after the strippers and before porn. Tempest Storm and Betty Page and pasties and whips had been moved aside by pinups of pretty velvety girls in bikinis and shorty nighties. Magazines like *Meat, Punt, Playboy, Nugget, Quick,* and *Escapade* showed girls you could take home to Mother—if only they'd put on some clothes and deny it was their layout. People reeled with shock that Amo had an MA, posed nude, and was writing a novel. If it had remained on that harmless level, Amo might've enjoyed it.

Amo's private session turned out to be with mashed face, Marv. "What else you got costumewise?" he grouched.

Swallowing her distaste, Amo became instantly pleasant and willing. "Sheer negligee I think you'll like—black, French fishnet underwear, blue shorty nightie, body stocking."

"Okay, we'll start wid da French thing. I'm trying to hit da magazines."

"Good, that'll be fun, " said Amo as if he were a

professional she was pleased to be working with. Man—sell, sell, sell! Sometimes Amo thought she'd collapse from the sheer effort of putting out so much drivel. Modeling forced her to glue on a smile, to plaster her face with coy and cupcake cute. To be On. Her Southern childhood surfaced in her smile and made it fetching. It would be several years before the strain showed and it cracked wide open.

Amo came out in the fishnet and lavender lace, decked out more seductively than she'd ever been for a man of her own, for this hunk of beef she wouldn't let within ten feet of her. Literally ten; she stood five feet back on the paper, he five feet in front of its edge. If he moved up, she moved back. She couldn't afford to wear these costumes to bed; she had to keep them fresh and bright for jobs. After a while they were tainted with the business, and she didn't want to.

Gyrating, Amo saw blood-colored skin, red meaty arms; he looked like he worked in a slaughterhouse. "What business you in, Marv?"

"Produce b'iness." The cigar rolled wetly to the other side of his mouth.

Amo smiled for sympathy at Sy and the small fellow who'd stayed, and they smiled back with understanding, so she thought.

The hour over, Marv said, "Can I drop you anywheres?"

The man who'd stayed stepped in, "I've already been given the honor."

He hadn't, but he got it. A small melancholic

thick-glassed fellow who fidgeted, he won hands down. In the old Chevy, Amo said, "You saved me from the classic fate worse than death."

He blinked politely, densely. "Will you pose for me—at your apartment? I have a mail-order business." Everybody claimed to have a mail-order business.

"Sure, ————." She blocked his name entirely afterward. "Two hours for $50."

"Tonight?"

"No!" At night she worked on the Maruvian novel. She was already eager for a silent dinner, accompanied by Lessing tonight, a nap, and then from eleven till dawn she sweated at the writing. Sweated at honing her consciousness, time warping her imagination, image-ing out her mind to get it all into Words. Words—alien and small but vast with Earthly manipulation and impact, words that were like plump pillows and translucence, soaring and nit-picking, words that would do the things she wanted, that she couldn't do with life, that made a home for her homeless spirit. How she hated herself for being so ill-equipped as an Outsider for learning the game and insisting on playing this hardest of all games, she with her V.C.-P.R. stature and her Maruvian needs for validation. Yet it was the only way for Amo to expand within herself enough to oust the self-hatred caused by this very ambition. Why self-hatred? Amo asked herself. Because she feared she'd never never achieve it.

"Please," he shivered. "I'll make it $100."

The show was over; she was Off. "You'll have to phone me tomorrow." She always checked them out with Sy. She asked enough to feel safe, not so much that Sy suspected her of stealing a fish.

"Two hundred—please!"

"Don't be silly," she said impatiently.

His hand, dawdling along the back of the seat, moved idly up and down the back of her neck. She sat forward to lose it politely and directed him to the turn on West Fifty-funky off Eighth. He stopped in front of her apartment under the streetlamp.

When he tried to kiss her, Amo brushed him off inattentively. And he strangled her, right there under the streetlight. She would've laughed in disbelief but his fingers choked it off. His fingers were like steel cables tightening and she couldn't pry up even the tip of one. She looked desperately into his eyes—wide open, staring straight at her—and knew he didn't see her. The streetlamp spotlit his face.

She waved her arms. No one came. W.R. she thought, where are you? Help me, W.R. Help!

Must've blacked out because when she came to, ———— had her head crammed under the steering wheel. ———— was on the other side of the car, steel arms with steel fingers squeezing tighter, harder, his body stretched away from her. Amo struggled till her head was upright, staring into the steering wheel at the people strolling by. She tried to pull at his hands but her own had turned to sweat and she couldn't grip. Suddenly she knew she was fading. In less than thirty seconds he would succeed and she would die.

Chapter 2
Angel of This Oith

Amo had never faced a killer, didn't know how to defend, couldn't think. Fury possessed her and she went wild. Like a hooked fish pulling the boat about, she thrashed and kicked in sheer aimless rage till she toppled him over, and she was back on her side of the car, he pressing her head into the seat, she kicking frantically into the air till she kicked through the windshield and broke the glass.

She didn't know where she was, her eyes were closed. They both heard the windshield crack. He loosened his hands and blinked like somebody waking up.

In a tiny boy's voice he whimpered, "Amo, I'm sorry—I didn't mean—"

A man leaned his head in. "What's going on?"

Amo gasped for air. "Open—" she said, and he opened the door and helped her out of the car.

The car took off like a shot.

The man held her arm as she limped into Chubby's Bar, feet bleeding, holding a broken shoe. He went for paper towels and Amo collapsed in a booth. Customers formed a silent circle at a safe distance. The man wiped the blood off her feet and picked out pieces of glass. Dark features wavering over pale skin; that's all she saw as she sat up. He took her to Roosevelt Emergency in a cab.

W.R., she was thinking, where were you, W.R.?

"What's your name?" he asked.

"Amo—Coove. You?" She couldn't talk. She was almost in shock.

"Malachi Stein." He leaned her head against his shoulder. Dark blonde, layers of floppy tendrils as in Greek statues. One of those unbelievable bodies. Whomp, whomp. A sexy face but too angular; the kind that photographs well, rather like Colette disguised as a Barbie doll.

"Didn't you slam him in the balls?" asked the Doctor, a toughie.

"No," said Amo surprised.

"Taught my daughters that when they were fifteen."

"Wouldn't have worked," croaked Amo in a damaged whisper. "Kept his body away." So *that* was why he stretched away from her—so she couldn't get to him. She felt her throat; the sound was ruptured.

The Doctor picked glass out of Amo's legs and feet. She didn't feel it till he pried a big jagged chunk out of her heel, which yanked her all the way out of shock. The dark man smiled at her with lusty concern; what was his name?

"Why didn't you go for his eyes? You dig in here." The Doctor demonstrated by pressing Amo's eyes with his thumb. "One good flip and an eyeball'll go."

Amo pulled back—"I wasn't in the Service." Could she have gouged his eyes? No. At least she might've ripped his cheeks with her fingernails. That had occurred to her. Yes, and she hadn't done it because it would've hurt him too much.

The Doctor finished examining her neck. "The bruises will turn pretty rainbow colors. You'll have the world's worst sore throat but you'll live."

Back at her pad with Malachi Stein, they had a drink and she had a look at him—brown bullets of eyes, black wily wiggly brows and self-serving sexy black hair. A city face—slick, canny, and mobile. Good shoulders, lean; Amo could not tolerate fat on men. Nobody was fat on Maruvia, but then they didn't age either. They forgot A.M.O. conveniently though, didn't they, W.R.? No reply. W.R. never spoke in company.

"You look like a defrocked priest—or rabbi. Are you Irish or Jewish?" She choked with the effort.

"Riiiight." Malachi's face opened up.

"What do you do?"

"I'm a mass murderer."

She smiled. "I've seen your composite at the Post Office." She hoped he was not your average, good-looking, tall, money-making executive, lawyer, newscaster, who'd learned his lessons and was applying them like a good boy. Then disguised himself as a Truth Seeker at night.

Finally Amo phoned Sy at the Studio and Malachi did most of the explaining. Sy wanted Amo on the line.

"Pliz, pliz, don' call the cops. They close me

down—I be out of business," he added slyly, "and where you find such easy woik?"

The jars got dustier; nobody came in for candy anymore. The kids went to the stores that sprang up clean with the high rises. "Okay, Sy. You've got enough problems."

"You an angel, Amo—angel of this oith. That crumb bum, he never get past this door again."

Amo got the crumb's home and business addresses for her lawyer—Paul would do it, as a friend—and hung up. "Malachi, is it?"

He grinned because she was coming round.

"What do you suppose the crumb does for a living?"

Malachi shook his head playfully, as if he were in a starry-eyed daze from just looking at her.

"He's a local radio announcer."

"You'd think he'd get his fill."

She didn't respond. She had no strength left to get to know him.

"If you like, I'll go,"—he watched her eyes leap—"but you shouldn't be alone tonight." For once it was probably true.

He put his large shoulders around the tiny form that clutched onto him for dear life, or as if she wanted to break him in two. They rolled onto the bed, and rolled over and over. His black jeans and stalks of legs, her blue jeans and crushable neck.

"I'm so cold," Amo shivered. Frozen with fear, her avalanche of passion.

They made love, Amo numb and shaking now and then. She couldn't feel him at all. But she was afraid *not* to make love when he wanted to; she couldn't take another confrontation. Malachi was as much a stranger as the other, and seemed just as trustworthy.

It was not easy posing at Sy's the next Tuesday. Amo wore heavy makeup on her neck to hide the bruises, felt grim, played light. Amo was becoming an actress. Though Sy guarded it, she kept watching the entrance.

As she was leaving, a blurry little woman stopped her outside the door. The woman flapped her arms conducting a symphony of woe. She was Bernie's wife. That's it—Bernie! Bernie what?

"I didn't know he was married," Amo rasped.

"Please—don't think I blame you." Mrs. Bernie gripped her arms. When Amo told her the lawyer would sue, Mrs. B. groaned, "Oh my God, four mouths to feed—you can't do that—we have no money. If they know at the station, he'll be out. It's happened before. He'll lose this job and where will we be, I ask you?" Her eyes fairly swam.

"He's done this before?" Amo asked.

She hung her head. "Yes, yes."

"Christ, woman, he ought to be in a mental hospital."

"If they put him away again, what will happen to us? I watch him—I try to watch him all the time. He doesn't mean it. He just . . . can't help it. He wouldn't harm a fly, I swear to you."

"How can you live with him?"

"He's all I've got." Mrs. B. pushed back a lank

strand of hair, as if she were dealing with a child who wet his pants.

Amo's lawyer said they could get $2,000, Bernie offered $500, Amo told the lawyer to take it, and he said she was a sucker. Amo's lawyer, Paul, was angry because his daughter had been raped recently.

Hi ho, America today! Everybody failed. Do you suppose Bernie finally succeeded? But then Amo blocked out his last name so she'll never know.

Chapter 3
Shark's Teeth

Amo called W.R. She was so angry she simply sat and let the Wrist Radar splutter . . . splut . . . bawk . . . ploop . . . pleeeep. . . .

AMO: "Couldn't you have intervened?"

W.R.: "Ah ho. Ah ho ha." (Maruvian laughter.) "Are you picking up on that God routine?"

AMO: "Well, no, but—"

W.R.: "Listen, we leave it to *you.* You volunteered, after all."

AMO: "I *did?* I don't remember. . . ."

W.R.: "Always kvetching about the tiniest injustice—a real crime fighter. So we thought you could handle a truly unjust society . . . make a dent. But if—"

Amo switched off in a rage.

W.R. called back. "Rage on."

AMO: "Okay, W.R. I'll give it to you like it is—here. Why did you have to make me so small and overendowed, as they call it? They think that's sexy looking. Sex—they can't see past it, some people. Why did you make me a woman at all?"

W.R.: "What on Earth is the difference?"

AMO: "On Earth—plenty. Maruvian woman is not the same as Earthwoman. In size, I am to the average man as he is to a pro-football tackle."

W.R.: "So?"

AMO: "They like to attack smaller things. They start out squashing bugs and pulling legs off frogs and shooting birds. Then they beat up on the small people—they have school playgrounds for the purpose. Then, to the bar fights and off to wars to beat up small yellow people."

W.R.: "Why . . . why—?"

AMO: "Because we exist, we're small. We remind them of weakness. It's part of their training. Compete, push, aggress, dominate, possess . . . surely you remember reading about primitive days on Maruvia? How the losers beat up on the lost."

W.R. (sighing): "They're nowhere near Universal Peace then?"

AMO: "Shhhhhhh—catapulting to destruction like lovers. As if they were invulnerable, like the God they invented."

W.R.: "We've been pacific and equal for so long—it's hard for me to grasp these primordial feelings."

AMO: "For me, too. Do you realize, W.R., that I *did not want to hurt* the man who was killing me?"

W.R.: "Yes! Yes, that worried us—a lot."

AMO: "It was sheer instinct, W.R. I couldn't help it."

W.R.: "I know."

AMO: "I didn't want to cause him pain."

W.R.: "Our finest Maruvian characteristic—*feeling for others as much as you feel for yourself.* We thought it would be a great benefit there—the Interconsciousness System."

AMO: "But *they* don't have it."

W.R.: "Maybe we should've given you shark's teeth instead."

AMO (after a pause): "Precisely my meaning, W.R."

Chapter 4
A Typical Maruvian Girl

"Tell me your fantasies, Wonder Nut," Malachi chirruped.

"Malachi, it . . . sounds like the phone's tapped."

"Sure, it is. Sounds like an echo chamber, right?"

"But, *why?*"

"Well, the FBI has a caseload so they tap my phone. And every once in awhile they come by and steal my mail to see what I'm up to."

"You sound so casual."

"What the hell." Malachi was somewhere Left, an activist if not a revolutionary, depending on the weather. With an ex-rabbi father and an ex-nun mother, he was born confronted. He *was* almost a defrocked priest; he'd quit the priesthood in his last year in seminary. Now he struggled along as a photographer and studied acting with Uta Hagen at HB Studio. His own studio was a garment center loft, off Sixth on Thirty-first street. He would talk to her about politics only in generalities. She probed and he evaded.

"You're not doing anything subversive?" She gave it

the Miss Goody Two-Shoes tone for the man with his
ear to the mike.

Malachi roared, cackled, coughed. "Raise my right
hand, I'm sincerely yours, Nonviolent, Sir." Then
soberly, "No, I am."

"That's good to know," Amo's voice lightened.

"What are you wearing?"

"A sweater I copped from a fella and jeans."

"That doesn't help my hard-on any. I was scheming
you naked." Malachi took great pride in his organ, as
monumental as his ego. Mal had to do absolutely
nothing to merit his own highest esteem and he often
wondered that other people had to work so hard at it.
Take Amo—she seemed to feel a sense of mission that
she could not fulfill, as if she were constantly
disappointing some higher power. It never occurred to
him that she could be superior without being
egocentric, and why.

Being committed politically, Malachi felt morally
superior; he'd transcended his balking heritage.
Besides its obvious validity to him, it solved his
personal problems—it was a selfless ego trip. Then,
the acting involved him creatively just as he was losing
interest in photography, and if that didn't work out,
he'd find something else. Amo's creative demands
seemed much more imperative: she *had* to write the
novel just as she *had* to dismiss the modeling. She was
as anxious about it all as he was relaxed. She wrote
surprisingly well, considering, especially the Maruvian fantasies and the New York Stories, as she called
them. Mal thought it strange that Amo was still having

strangulation dreams. She'd find herself trapped under the bedcovers, unable to breathe, suffocating.

"Next time you phone," said Amo, "I'll rip my clothes off into the receiver." She mouthed a sound of buttons popping and scraped her fingernails over the mouthpiece. "Ziiiiiiippppp!"

Malachi said petulantly, "You haven't told me a fantasy."

"In the middle of the day? That's obscene." They really got along very well; buffet and banter, most relaxing. Though Amo often felt it was his defense against revealing more of himself.

"Hopefully."

"Wait—I'll get something I wrote last night about Mah Early Lahf in the Big City." She rummaged about the desk top and returned. "Ready?"

"It better be short and sexy."

"Okay, ahem," she paused. "Willow is thinking this—the antiheroine, I should say." She paused again to assume a reading voice.

"'Willow was a typical New York girl sleeping around with everybody in town. She didn't do it because it was good or great or anything like that, or because it was bad and evil and delicious, but because it was the only thing to do. Not just in the fashionable sense. Everybody did it and either you went along or you got none, and Willow was too horny for that. There was a time when she would've settled down with any number of men—one at a time, that is—but they all scooted right along to the next girl, barely remembering they'd slept with her last night or last week or the week before, when she saw them at the next party. Willow knew they remembered literally but didn't recall actually—she'd look at them very closely, inquiringly, and they'd blush. When she was quite young, she looked at them with hatred and anger but that was long past.

"'Obviously there was something *wrong* with her. She discovered her heretical error: she wasn't with it. She got with it and became a cocksman herself. It was much more relaxing. She took them on as fast as they came. Always a sexual presence at parties, she no longer looked starved about the eyes but calmly lustful and greedy: a *conquistadora*. Her huge breasts no longer seemed to quake before assault but swelled with power, elbowed about with authority. Her dark hair coiled about her ears and caressed her neck. It did no good for Jim to call and say, "Hi, it's Jim." She might've slept with three Jims in the past month. Everybody had to identify himself; she couldn't remember voices.

"'She thought of herself as a grand *cocotte*, a latter-day *hetaera*. The men thought of her as a great seductress whom no one man could tame. "One man will never be enough for you, Willow," they told her. She smiled indulgently. Too much or too little, that was the story of her life. She didn't know how generous she was. She didn't know what else to do.'"

"*That's* not a fantasy—that's psychological," Malachi complained.

"But how do you like it?" Amo said meekly,

quaking, furious with herself for revealing weakness
and failure.

"I don't know." Troubled silence. "Depends on
what you're planning to do with it." Another silence as
she waited. "I don't know how broads think."

"You and your narrow-gauge emotional range." The
raging author. "Don't you *want* to know?"

"You don't understand your power, Amo." She used
it—made a living from it—but seemed unaware of it.
She played her wit against it and appeared formidable.
"You're a gutsy chick. You frighten men."

"What does that mean?"

"Uh-oh, other phone's ringing. Do me a favor
tonight, don't wear any panties."

"How can I, when you're zeroing in?"

"No, I mean when we go to dinner, okay?"

"Why—?"

"Turns me on. *Ciao,* baby."

That was not what Amo called power. Gingerly, she
felt her throat.

The dear old dump on West Fifty-funky was
unhesitatingly the crummiest building from river to
river. During Amo's long-term sentence there, it
peeled, shredded, corroded, and caved with nary a
glance from the owners. The stairs dangled, the
banisters were not to be touched by human hand.
However, at $64–$85 a month, the tenants bore up. On
third were Amo and Iya, the ballet dancer. Amo
wanted to be friends but Iya disapproved of Amo's

nude modeling. Amo disapproved of many of the models because they'd do anything for money, if it was enough. But she understood why; they were all pressured. Below Amo and Iya were an electric guitarist and an anarchist who always had a working girl friend; various single men in the unspeakable single rooms; and Mr. O'Donovan the Super, a retired lawyer who chain-smoked and was dying of lung cancer.

Bounded by CBS and Carnegie Hall, the tacky show biz neighborhood had a wary feel of camaraderie. Folks nodded at each other on the street, as if to say *they* (the square world) think we're failures but *we* know there's always hope.

Into Amo's pleasure palace at the dinner hour strode estimable Malachi Stein with his standard Saturday night hard-on.

They embraced and Amo pinched his chin with great seriousness. "Do you carry that uptown in a sling?" Amo couldn't tolerate men who didn't try to do something worthwhile with their lives. Which eliminated all Earthmen but artists and moralists of one stripe or another. In the primitive days Maruvia had saved itself when the Gobblers had knocked each other off in wars, still finally only humble idealists were left. Now that their lives involved helping each other, the Maruvians were relatively happy.

Malachi kissed her and rubbed against her till she pulled away. When he smiled, his rosy underlip showed like a bubbly boy, wet and friendly. His mouth was very open, teeth very many. It amused Amo to decide which of his features were Irish, which Jewish. His mouth was Irish, eyes Jewish—brooding and heavy but for the maniacal spark. Or vice versa. His pale translucent skin had a boyish texture; the heavy black hairs appeared glued one. Though his face always seemed ready to take off in glee, he was a very private man. When pressured, he responded with even more sexuality and gaiety, but not with Malachi. With perception but not revelation or need. Perhaps his best characteristic was that Mal wanted to see her every week, week in and week out. Everybody wanted to sleep with Amo; few bothered to say.

Amo fixed tequila with lime before the phone rang, which it was prone to do. "'lo."

"Is this Miss Amo Coove, the model?" asked a light sweet male voice.

"Yep."

"Um, I was just wondering—does your family know what you're doing?"

"No, why don't you call and tell them?" Amo talked to so many strangers every day that she felt like a camp counselor in a tent on Times Square.

"I mean," the high mournful voice persisted, "how do you hide the magazines from them?"

Amo gave Malachi an exhausted eye and he brought over her drink. "I don't broadcast it, that's all."

"What does your boy friend think?"

"He thinks it's . . . sweet." Her eyes danced at Malachi.

"But if he loves you, doesn't he care—?"

"Who are you?"

"Tommy Elbert is my name."

"How old are you, Tommy?"

"Thirteen."

"Aren't you a little young to be looking at pinup magazines?"

"Aren't you a little young to pose for them?" he countered. "Are you sixteen?"

Amo laughed. "Tommy, if you can read, you'll see I'm twenty-six."

"Oh." Hurt, momentarily. "Could I . . . you think I could meet you sometime?"

"Tommy, I have a boy friend."

"But he doesn't care about you like I do."

"Maybe not, Tommy, maybe not. But I have to hang up now."

"Oh, please—" he sort of whinnied.

"You call another time. 'Bye now." Amo hung up the phone and leaped onto Malachi's lap at the marble café table which constituted the living room. Since it was a one-room apartment, the desk was the studio, the double bed the bedroom, the bookcase the library. The kitchen had been a closet and the bathroom with lion's-paw tub an old pantry. Amo constantly measured the room to try to make it bigger. It was exactly 17½ by 13½. Outside the splintered windows, New York roared and joggled by on wheels, spewing exhaust to add to the cannonade from the smokestack across the street. If Amo didn't slam the window when the wind changed, black smoke swarmed in.

"Here's to Saturday night, luv." Malachi hugged her.

"*Salud, chulo.*" Their faces batted a daffy joy back and forth.

The phone rang again. "'lo."

"This Amo Coove?"

"Right the first time."

The man commenced to breathe like a steam engine, evidently masturbating. "I'm sucking your cunt right now," he informed her.

Amo dropped the phone as if stung, told Mal.

He grabbed the phone. "Leave my wife alone, you motherfucker," he roared, slammed it down.

"Fans, they call them," said Amo.

"Get out of the phone book, I keep telling you."

"You know I can't. I'm a business, just like you are."

The phone rang again. "Maruvia must be descendent," Amo said. "All the kooks are out."

"Let's get out of here," Mal said, annoyed. "No, better yet, I'll go down on you while it rings." He dove for her, the phone pealed on.

It must've stopped at some point but they were not aware of it. His lips were so juicy, his tongue so hot, then at the crucial moment with celestial timing, he pressed the mere tip of his finger toward the back and she came like a fountain.

"You're always making me come before dinner," Amo said, disarrayed and saphappy, the room filled with their fleshy sparkle.

Chapter 5
S-M Jockey and Steed

They ate at the Ninth Circle, Malachi vaguely scouting for new models. Dark, masochistically jammed, filled with up-to-the-second people craning their necks for artists.

"Hey, I sold the color in the crochet bikini again," Mal said.

"Great, babe. How much did we make?" She posed for him free and they split the loot from the magazines.

"Only $250—second rights aren't worth much."

"I'll take it. Which one?"

"Punt"

"Oh yeah."

"Heard from *Meat* about being Tidbit of the Month?"

"Not yet."

Neither of them was really interested except for the support it provided. "If you had a really great face, we could make a mint."

"Sorry. I try."

"You photograph better than you look."

"Everybody says that," said Amo. Amo looked

pretty good on Earth to the camera eye, though she could walk down the street without turning a head. The camera caressed her skin, glowed her eyes, and told her she was beautiful, desirable. Then people seemed to think so. Not Amo, of course; she knew better.

"It's the smile," said Mal. "Fantastic empathy, like a tuning fork."

It's the Interconsciousness System, thought Amo. "How was the community turnout at the demonstration?"

"Great, man—loaded, the whole block. They're finally learning political organization." He ran liaison between black and radical activist groups.

"Thanks to the grrreat leader." Right or wrong, she esteemed his idealism.

"Somebody has to do it."

"Let's talk about your activities."

"Let's not." Malachi went stolid.

Salad bowl, black bread came. They served themselves, taking all the cherry tomatoes.

His dour pout lifted, eyes twinked. "Did you remember to not wear your panties?"

Amo snapped her fingers. "Shoot, I forgot and wore them."

He shook a playful finger at her. "We'll have to punish you for that later."

"Pretend I'm a great white fluffy dog." They were in Mal's double bed in the cavernous loft with its white white walls, hiding from all the pictured people, places, and products. "A montrous white dog raping you."

Amo laughed hysterically. "I don't mean to disappoint you but I'd prefer a swan. Large white dogs don't turn me on."

"Auburn ones?"

"Come on, *Malisimo.*"

"There was this silky female setter the summer I was eleven on the farm. I screwed her regularly." His arms were behind his head, face full of easy boyish confidences.

"Was she good?" Amo was disgusted but not sure she should be; after all, he was a child of Earth. Some kid.

"Well . . . at that age, I thought so."

"You're putting me on, aren't you?" Her face was befuddled.

"No," he said, large-eyed and trusting, brushing his palm over her nipples, then giving them a twist. "Then there was the black I met in the grocery store. I brought him up here and let him screw me in the ass. Then afterward, he wanted to kiss me—yuk!"

"Naturally," said Amo.

"I'm no homosexual," Mal objected. "I just wanted the experience."

She hated him when he did this—turned her on with shock and sensation rather than affection. Sometimes she just turned her back, then he laughed and apologized. Other times it worked—if she could force herself to shift gears. Which she did out of *affection,* since he seemed to need this mechanical byplay, this guided tour to the perversities. This time she stopped him. "Why can't we just *touch* to turn on?"

"Artifice is everything, pet."

"*Why?*"

"It's fun."

He rolled over, enclosed and lifted one breast in his large hand, and sucked it hard. The nipple grew half an inch. Then he nuzzled his head between and hugged them to his cheeks and honked like a seal.

"Sit on my face," he said and lifted her into place.

"That's—" Vulgar, she started to say, eyes wild as she stared down into his, above the brown-blonde mustache he'd suddenly sprouted. "Beautiful . . . beautiful," she swayed.

He tilted her forward and back so he wouldn't miss any orifice or nodule. She came on his face and blushed. She scampered down his belly and sat on his large hooked organ, grinding blissfully away. Opening her eyes, she saw a look on Mal's face that could only be called adoration. He dropped it instantly when observed. Leaned forward and he took both her tips in his mouth. High as addicts, they came, first Amo because she could come in long waves and liked to pull the chain of orgasm out of him, then Mal, both quaking, gasping, moaning.

"Answer to a Maruvian's prayer, you are." Amo luxuriated in the sheets, kissed his cheek reverently.

"Always suspected it, Wonder Nut," he grinned joyfully.

Exhilarating—what a relief to let it all out, the full range of her sexuality, without politeness. She got out of bed, cupped her breasts, and jumped up and down hard four or five times, as he laughed.

"Hope everything comes out all right," he said, as she hopped off. Then, too late, he remembered the whip.

The jumping was to start the sap so that when she went to the bathroom, it would meander out. Amo had taken herself off the Pill and gone back to her trusty diaphragm. She liked to watch the big fat gluey globs fall in the water. You could almost judge Earthmen by the quality of their semen. If it was thick liquid and lots of it, they were good lovers. If it was thick near solid, they suffered constipation of the senses. If it was thin and watery, they suffered premature ejaculation.

Mal and Amo looked at color slides, one batch of Mommy and Sonny looking saintly for aspirin, the other of Amo on round and king-size beds for a bedding chain. They smoked a joint while sipping Chilean Chablis, both in bikini underwear.

"I forgot to punish you for wearing panties," Mal said, and took a little thonged whip out of the prop closet and began slapping it against his thigh.

Amo stared and backed away.

"Lie down now and I'm going to spank you for being a bad girl." He was convulsed with laughter. "A bad girl for letting me scwew her." Baby talk tone, "Bery bery bad." He flapped the whip gently against her bottom. "Lie down now and Daddy's going to punish you."

Holding her throat, Amo stumbled backward toward the bed.

"Oh God, Amo, it's just a game. I won't hurt you."
Eyes large and helpless.

She crossed her arms to steady herself. "Guerrilla
theater at bedtime?" It hurt to want love, humanity—and get this sideshow.

Mal tripped her onto the bed and flipped her over,
backside up, hit her lightly with the whip that barely
felt. Amo didn't know whether she was anaesthetized
with fear or whether he was really gentle. But tears
came to her eyes. "You're trying to humiliate me."

"No, I'm not. Now you do it to me." He knelt dog
fashion, most unappetizingly.

She hit him. The little thongs flicked against his
softest flesh. She hit him harder because she was
angry.

"No—don't hurt. It's only a game," he smiled
encouragingly.

"I don't like sado-masochistic fun." She flicked it
against him, rather bored.

He rolled over. "You have to get with the fantasy,
that's all. You release your repressions—to intensify
reality. To get at truth."

"But my *life* is fantasy. Did I tell you what I got in
the mail this morning? A rubber—in a note saying,
'From Big Boy, A Fan.'" She handed him the whip.
"What do I need this for?"

She noticed he was hard again. "That's a good
fantasy. Why didn't you tell me that one?"

"Because it's true." Suddenly Amo whistled like a
police siren. "Commie pinkos—black bastards—moth-
erfuckin' hippies!" She demonstrated on various sides.

"*Sieg heil, sieg heil.* Off the fuzz—*sieg heil.*"

He raised the whip, eyes black nuggets.

"You can't control it, see," said Amo calmly. "You're acting out your fear of the fuzz. Maybe it was worse than you told me?"

Mal slumped slightly. "Nobody likes to be hit."

She put her arms around him. "Why don't you tell me?"

"It was a year ago. I've wanted to smash something ever since," he mumbled, voice muffled by her soothing breast. "I feel so . . . deballed."

They hugged each other. After awhile she said softly, "It doesn't do any good to pass it on, though."

Malachi was hurt. "I wasn't! That was erotic play. You're making it ugly."

He hit her lightly with the whip and she forced a smile and said, "I'm sorry."

And he was hard again. She sat on his lap, all the way down on it, and he hit her lightly with the floppy thongs. Don't be chicken, Amo, be Maruvian; you're here to explore Earth life. Very lightly till she said, "Harder," and he increased it little by little as she galloped for the finish line. But she was so numb with fright that she couldn't tell how hard he was hitting her. He just kept smiling. Then they reversed positions, Mal on top, and she whipped him. With her short arms and his 175 pounds on her, it was a lot of work. He swooned in no time, and they came in neck and neck, the large jockey and his tiny steed.

In the dressing room mirror, spotlit by light bulbs, she was surprised to see deep red slashes on her fanny, which began to burn. On his too. What were they doing, did they know?

When she saw the red prison stripes, Amo knew. She remembered high school in Atlanta when she and her boy friend would go out to the lake to play around and the cops would roar up and flash lights into the car. "Where're the cops?" they'd say if the cops didn't show, trembling with delight, turned on by threat, unable to get to Third Base, their stopping point. All the turn-on fears—the cops, denial, violence for love.

Amo wouldn't do it again. Mal said she was square.

Chapter 6
Mono Love

W.R.: "Thanks, A.M.O. That was great for my class."

AMO: "Class, W.R.? What's up?"

W.R. (sigh): "The Earth TV and movies have become surprisingly popular. You know, the Cult of the Happy Primitive. And people—not the brightest, you understand—are yearning for Couple Love, Mono Love—they have many names for it. They don't realize how power oriented it is. So I showed my class your . . . jockey and steed engagement."

AMO (breathless): "Well, I don't know if I like that much exposure. Did you get that dear man, what's his name, the Human Choker?"

W.R.: "Ahm, yes, we did. That was Lesson Number One. Don't be angry now."

AMO: "Was it useful, W.R.?"

W.R.: "Very."

AMO: "Well, if I can't help myself, I'd like my people to get something out of all this."

W.R.: "We were hoping you'd see it that way."

Chapter 7
Miracle of the Flesh

Amo was flying to California to pose as Tidbit of the Month for *Meat* magazine, which would publish a short story of hers in the same issue. Amo hoped it would be a breakthrough for her, this being a Tidbit as well. Mal kissed her good-bye at the East Side Airlines Terminal, whispered, "Be sure and sleep with him so you can tell me about it." He gave her the cutest imp eye.

"How about leaving it to me?" Amo stuck her tongue tip at him and jumped on the bus to LaGuardia. All part of Malachi's high moral code of complete faithlessness that he'd devised for the two of them. Hard to beat that total-freedom rap.

Met at the airport by himself, Pelfrick Pedlar, famous swinging publisher of *Meat*. A short man with a Valentino gigolo face, wearing a dark suit, Frick opened the door to the limo like a funeral director, all middle-class propriety and rigidity.

"You act like an American gothic," Amo said, surprised.

"Heh, heh," laughed Frick, "nobody ever said that to me." His smile lifted like a stiff curtain, then fell with a thud.

They ate dinner at the Meat Den. The management kept running over paying court. Frick this, Frick that; his name was bandied about on all sides. Tidbits who waited on tables wiggled over, smiling unctuously. In their tight costumes they looked like stuffed sausages link-tied at the waist. The king was in his court.

Amo had a Bloody Mary, Frick a Dr. Pepper. Teeth clamped on cigarillo, he seemed to bite on his words. "Hard-hitting story for a girl."

"Thanks." Amo's cat eyes softened womanishly when someone liked her writing. Her claim to literary fame rested so far on two published short stories, one lately anthologized, amazingly, with Fitzgerald and Mary McCarthy. This was the third.

"You write like a man."

"I write like a Maruv—like myself," she smiled, noticing the eyes glued on herself and the hometown hero. "Run for Congress while it lasts," she said.

"Lasts—?" Frick removed the cigarillo, incredulous, and fixed on her his dead-earnest preacher's glare. "I can't understand why you're not more impressed with our operation."

"All through bouncing boobies," Amo mused. "The miracle of the flesh."

Cigarillo clamped back in, Frick puffed, "The nude body is beautiful. There's nothing dirty about it."

"Agreed," Amo shrugged. "But you exploit it."

Frick was amused. "That's why you're here."

Always dying to fling their clothes aside and blame some man for it.

"I exploit it too—that's what you're saying?"

"Think about it." The hooded eye treatment, smokescreen hurtling upward.

Amo twirled the Bloody. "I'm buying time—you're trying to build a business. I *hope* it's not the same." She reached into her Mexican bag and dug out a musty literary magazine, that looked as if it had never seen the light of day, and a slick paperback anthology with her previously published stories.

"Uh huh." Frick handled them as a rich man does small change, lifted a grin, and passed them back.

The next morning at the studio, gray glare pushed at the windows. The photographer, Hans, a tall stooped old Dutchman, was testing his color film; his assistant, a leering Italian gnome, leered at Amo. An earnest young black, Josh, so far represented editorial *Meat*. In the dressing room Jan the stylist, who looked more like a model than Amo, applied pancake makeup to the back of Miss Amo Coove, Tidbit of the Month for March, 196–. Frick wasn't around.

Amo herself coated the front of her body. The purpose, said Jan, was to give uniform skin texture like a body stocking. It did that, Amo agreed, but it also flattened form and eliminated curves. Normally she used makeup only on her face and neck, her knees, and the broken vein like a jagged radar signal on the inside of her wrist. She aroused her nipples and emphasized her cleavage with Vaseline. Jan suggested a bit of pink lipstick on the nipples but Amo held firm. "I don't want to look like a candy store."

"But you're Miss Tidbit. We want you to look delectable," Jan pouted.

"I'm a writer," Amo cracked. Where was Frick, wasn't he coming?

Jan's eyes grew, "We never had a writing Tidbit." She pinned a little chignon of ringlets on top of Amo's mass of dark blonde hair.

"Don't you think that's redundant?"

"What—?" Jan thrust her chin anxiously forward.

"Looks gorgeous, Jan. You're doing a great job." Amo slid into the negligee and boudoir slippers provided by *Meat.*

"We're ready," Jan shouted and another girl, Mary Ann, ran in.

Amo marched from the dressing room to the shooting area surrounded by Jan and Mary Ann, who shielded her from the coarse stares of nonexistent passersby. The gnome wiped off the soles of her slippers with a damp cloth so they wouldn't leave prints on the pink paper backdrop. Jan asked Hans if he wanted the negligee on and he shook his head, of course, so Jan removed it from Amo's shoulders as if she were unveiling the Kohinoor diamond. Everybody was terribly deferential. A nude shot, especially Tidbit of the Month, is a solemn, grand, even slightly dangerous occasion.

Silence, as Amo faced them head on and climbed onto the bed that constituted the set. Where was Frick, didn't he want to see? Amo sat on the downy bed covered with a blue blanket which was draped low around her hips. There were male artifacts about—shoes under the bed, a jacket and tie. The *Meat* logo featured over the headboard was a Tidbit abstract—female breasts as seen from above, or the letter *M* rounded out with nipples on it.

The scene was to be a pillow fight between Amo and unseen implied male lover. Lights on: Hans mutters something, gnome moves a light. Hair light bounces over Amo's head casting shadows; they they inch it back.

In bustles Frick, talking busily with his ad director, a tall curly second lead. Amo's tits stuck out like early-warning devices but she pretended she didn't notice. When he said hello, her whole body blushed. That had happened only once before, when she first posed for Malachi.

Frick said casually, "Well, you look as good as your pictures. This is Wade Graves, our ad manager."

Nude but for the hip swaddling, Amo said, "How do you do?"

Wade, "Hi there."

Frick to Wade, "Not bad for a writer."

Wade, "Not a bit."

How voracious the gazes, hers included. Amo pulled back, reeling, and basked in a sunbath of lust and hot lights.

"Where's your Phi Bete key?" Frick asked.

"Stolen, when I was robbed."

"Here's one to wear."

"I don't want to. That looks cheap."

"It's very elegant camp." He clasped the key necklace round her neck, the gold key dangling like a cross between the breasts of a Puerto Rican whore.

"Ready, Frick?" asked Hans.

Frick nodded, stopped sucking his brown cigarillo, and the shooting began. Frick and Wade threw feathers to simulate the pillow fight. Amo arched her back extremely, lifted the pillow which also lifted her breasts, smiled rampagingly, and threatened to throw. She held it there, camera clicked, and feathers flew.

Feathers flew *after* the camera clicked. They did it again. Feathers flew before. Again. After. Again. Before. Again—kachoo! Feathers in Amo's nose. Amo jiggles with laughter and feathery hair. Feathers fly backward and land all over Frick and Wade (wind conditions change as result of air conditioner churning on). Kachoo—wahhhhcchhooooo—ha—ha—ha—choooooooo, Frick and Wade sneeze. Everyone falls about laughing. Amo laughs so hard she collapses like a tower mangled in bedwear. Frick and Wade sag against the walls.

"Serious now—serious, everybody," old Hans tries. Jan and Mary Ann cluck about.

Amo's face glistens with sweat and bits of feathers. "Oh, really," says Mary Ann and begins picking them off and mopping her with a powder puff. Jan recombs her hair. Amo checks it seriously in hand mirror, giggling in spurts, catches Frick's eye and both snortle helplessly.

"Okay, everybody," says Hans. "Vunce more."

"Here we go, gang," says Frick and they went to work again. Amo arched, smiled, lifted the menacing pillow, and the boys tossed feathers on target. She tried other angles. Amo's body had gone public; she thought of it now as her commercial entity. Up on her knees, she bent forward so her breast beacons looked fuller. She squeezed them together by holding the pillow out to the side like a baseball bat. She put the pillow underneath and lifted them like a shelf, a display shelf. She knew this game—lit beacons —backward.

They finished with the *Meat* shot. Most readers don't understand how it is accomplished. Simple— they cut off the girl's head. Not really. They merely lean it all the way off a bed and place a tiny camera on her chin and shoot down from there onto the M-scape of mountainous snowy dairy whips. The Phi Bete key hung awry.

"That should do it," said Hans. "We'll do another setup after lunch."

Eyes aslash, Amo slammed the pillow at Frick, who zapped it back. Wade emptied the bag of feathers on Amo, who slung the pillow at both advancing men before diving under the blue blanket.

As their heads emerged from under the blue blanket, Amo was scampering off to the dressing room with Jan and Mary Ann. "Those kids still play Tent," she chirped.

Chapter 8
Charles Atlas of the Sex World

Frick's suite with its huge round bed looked like a movie studio surrounding a lost island. A floating bed where two tiny figures huddled against the technological storm on the walls, abutting the bed, about to sink it. Although she was in it, Amo couldn't decide whether she wanted to go to bed with him or not. She lounged in a Nepalese robe, he in one from Karachi, that were part of the decor. She couldn't even feel guilty because Mal didn't care. Or said he didn't. She almost thought she wouldn't. She was tired of playing Scheherazade for Malachi, bringing him new tales every week.

"How'd you get to be a writer"—Frick chewed on cigarillo—"a sexy little big-titted entrée like you?"

"Shoot, you believe your publicity! How'd you get to be a *Meat* publisher?"

"That's how. I create it—I *am* it—and I take no small pride in the fact." He fiddled with dials and lights and apertures. "Let's watch movies."

Psychedelic patterns and images cavorted on two screens and the wall behind the bed. Image-weary

Amo tried to duck them. They made her squirm and feel buggy.

"Yessirree, I'm rather proud of *Meat*. *Meat* has changed my life," he spoke as from the lecturn. "I live the ideal existence of the urban bachelor. Here in my lair during the week and on weekends I drop in on the wife and kids."

"You're married?" She'd never heard that.

Suck, suck on damp cigarillo. "Don't you find married men attractive?"

"They're taken."

"That's how I figured it. How could I be a married swinger? It destroys the image. Free and swinging, not trapped—that's the image."

Amo tried to be helpful. "Use Wade for your stick figure."

Frick smiled tightly. *"I'm* the publisher. Wade works for *me."*

"Get a divorce and play the swinging *Meat*ball, then." She leaned over to get a peek at his chest under the robe.

"Exactly what I did—heh, heh." Frick scowled through laughter at her presumption. "The marriage was bad almost from the start."

"Sounds familiar." Amo had been considering Living Together lately, thinking of proposing to Mal the *macho malo*. Straighten him out. Enough of this standard Saturday night stuff.

Frick stared up at the smoked mirror on the ceiling that gave him back the image of the ideal urban bachelor. "Now that I've got *Meat* she wants me back.

Now that I've pulled away and got some better stuff going. When we were first married—she wouldn't even *sleep* with me before we were married—she didn't like it any too well. Finally I got tired of it all and got a girl friend on the side. Then all of a sudden, she wanted me. Are all women like that?" He rolled over to peek up her robe.

"Those kind are—the non-sensual. They're turned on by jealousy." Was it real, this appealing naïveté?

On his elbows he laughed his nervous heh-heh. "Used to be, I couldn't make out for trying. In high school—even in college, *no*body'd sleep with me—not even my fianceé. *Meat* changed my life, all right."

"The Charles Atlas of the sex world," exclaimed Amo. "From ninety-pound weakling to sex bomb overnight."

"You do have a weird wit." He got up and played with the dials, changing the movies, sat with his arm around her under the robe. The title came on the first screen, *The Red Dog,* in black and white. "Sort of a classic," he explained. On the second screen in color, *Switcheroo.*

Whatever Amo expected, it was not a tough plumpish whore trying to entice a supposedly red dog to screw her. "A dirty movie!" she said, startled. *Switcheroo* appeared to be an orgy full of pretty people by a swimming pool.

"Don't you like authentic stag films?" Frick casually sucked the cigarillo, stroked his organ under the robe.

"Not now." She stared in attentive shock.

"Especially now." He reached for her hand and put it on his growing organ. "They'll arouse you."

She yanked her hand back. "There are other ways." She crossed her arms angrily, and watched the whore trying to get the red dog to approach her vagina. The dog appeared perfectly satisfied with her kneecap. In *Switcheroo* two couples were madly eating their partners. Back to *The Red Dog,* who was most uncooperative. But that great old show biz spirit prevailed and the lady—who evidently wanted her pay—proceeded to do it to herself with an enormous dildo. Back to *Switcheroo,* where the little couples' heads would come up, harkening to directions from the director. They would switch instantly to another part of the same body or another body. Flick, flick with the tongue. Heads up again to listen. Switch again.

Amo laughed so hard she fell off the bed. It turned her on though, sort of raced her motor to non-specific generic greed.

Frick scowled; "That's supposed to be sexy." He was as displeased with her levity as she was with his lack of tenderness. He wanted cold sex and she wouldn't give it; she wanted passion and he wouldn't give it.

Amo squinted at *Switcheroo.* "Who's that man in the blond wig—is that you?"

He showed no shock. "Of course not," he said mildly.

The next time he reached for her hand and embraced his organ with it, she was curious and disliked him enough to start playing it, and after awhile he rolled over and started kissing her breasts. Though not as large as Mal, he was quite substantial and provided a hard undeviating plunge, rhythm as unvaried as a metronome.

Promptly at three P.M. the next afternoon they wended their way back to the *Meat* office and as if it were company policy, Frick introduced Amo to several top dogs before they went to lunch. Not till she was flying back to New York did it occur to Amo to wonder if, with all those apertures on the wall, she had been filmed in bed with Frick, the unsuspecting star of a new blue flick.

By the time she reached New York, Amo decided that was paranoid. Past the garbage cans and into the D.O.D. (Dear Old Dump), which looked not at all like the ideal Tidbit's hangout. The phone rang and it was Cesare from Milan, an Italian duke she'd gone with when he was a corporal in the U.S. Army. They had a swinging swooning reunion—out to dinner, home to bed. A swooping double bed whose broken springs they tried to curl around, the working Duke and the writing Tidbit. Next day he flew home to his wife and Amo called Mal (Wittgen) Stein.

She received a tight note from an editor she hadn't met saying they did not want any woman writer's name associated with *Meat,* and she should not expect them to publish her at all. Amo wrote Frick. He didn't answer. He was never there when she phoned. Amo's friendship with Frick disappeared.

Chapter 9
Click

The Great Minor Celebrity appeared. Amo's agent sold the story *Meat* rejected to the *Partisan Review*. When the March *Meat* came out, Amo became a Famous Body who was also a Serious Writer, your popular beauty & brains combo. Fan mail piled up, the phone rang incessantly. The bells of the city pealed for this month's instant celebrity.

The *Daily News* interviewed her: "Why a Phi Bete Posed in the Buff," shrieked the headline above a photo of Amo next to Brigitte and Sophia. Three times she appeared as Earl's Girl in Earl Wilson's column though she never met the man. Book publishers called. They called her a discovery, took her to lunch, flirted, and asked to see her novel when she had enough to show. This was what Amo really wanted. She went on the *Tonight Show*. When Johnny asked her opinion of *Meat*, she let out her anger at being excluded: "It's a private dining club for boys where the specialty is breast of Tidbit."

During the next year, a Happenings composer wrote a piece about her called *Amo Coove in 48 Seconds* that

Schonberg reviewed in the *Times*. She was queen of
the Hi-Fidelity Show at the Coliseum. Click, click
with discs. Decked out in a black bathing suit and a
million dollars worth of Harry Winston diamonds, she
was lifted aloft in an elephant's trunk to celebrate—
click, click—the opening of the Circus. She became
Miss Minute Maid for the O.J. company and posed
—click—with the President of the Stock Exchange
when it went on the Big Board. She did shows with
Teddy Snowcrop, a dwarf who drove a Jaguar, and
Colonel Morton, a benign Russian Jew. They wanted
her to do their TV commercials. But when they tested
her voice, it seemed to have a strange undertone of
interference like a radar signal, or maybe it was the
Southern accent. Amo did silent TV commercials, one
where she was a Daisy Mae type who wrastled a gun
away from a Revenoo-er and tossed him a can of
mouthwash instead. They ran it for two years and she
collected residuals, which are conscience money.

Amo pitched hair dryers and contact lenses, pills
and pools in magazine ads. Lolled about record album
covers as Cleopatra and ground around as a belly
dancer. On paperback covers, stood proud as an
eighteenth-century courtesan and stooped wanton as a
nineteenth-century bar girl. Kissed and killed for the
media. She did a skit with Sammy Davis at a trade
show, starred in a nude scene in a Fellini movie. She
posed for space comics and science fiction books so
often that when anybody in the field wanted a model,
they thought of Amo without understanding why.

As time went on, Amo googoo-eyed and dollied the

boys from hundreds of pinup and men's magazines, and posed for most of the amateur photographers and camera clubs in the Northeast. Movie agents phoned, strippers' agents, pornographers. She made several movie tests but there was that voice problem, that reverberating echo already tuned to a distinctly different drummer, or frequency, as the case may be.

Limousines carried her to parties to meet princes who, it turned out, represented cosmetics firms or airlines. Society gents took her to charity balls and she appeared in the *Times*, pictured among the rich. She met Marlon Brando at Pavillon, Gore Vidal at the St. Regis, Cary Grant at Elmo's. With other models from the agency, she collected money in midtown for the Blind.

For years and years, phone calls and fan letters, mystical and profane. Voices tough and contemptuous, full of desire and filth—company presidents, unemployed blacks, rich architects, Servicemen, tremulous accountants, arrogant restaurant suppliers, uptight lawyers.

Also writers and actors and painters—Saul Bellow, Louis Gossett, Jack Carter, Philip Roth, Gardner McKay, José Luis Cuevas, Joseph Heller, Clay Felker, Steve McQueen. "I carried your picture in my battle helmet into the fighting in Vietnam," wrote an ex-Marine captain. She went with him to a peace rally in Central Park.

Most American males who flipped through magazines at newsstands knew her by name; most women had never heard of her. Amo was queen of the pinup magazines—fantasy courtesan of the media, visual substitute in the global village for the Old World fancy lady. Not that she'd planned it that way. All she wanted was a way to support her writing. An American career.

Malachi beside her, Amo hauled out the heavy modeling portfolio to put the new full-page New York *Times* ad in it. Mal had his first acting job, second lead in the Off-Off Broadway play in rehearsal, *Dirty Is Better.* Amo currently referred to him as our most promising Dirty Young Man.

"You're the high priestess of unobtainable sex," Mal declaimed. He checked the time. "Conservative estimates across the nation show two thousand men masturbating over your pictures at this very instant."

Howling, Amo stood up on the bed as he clutched her ankles and stared up at her with unctuous profundity. "I am the impossible vicarious woman, guardian of the mysteries." Then she felt ashamed. "Do many of them do that?"

"Amo—they phone you in the middle of it."

She blushed. "Somehow I figured it was three or four weirdos."

Mal considered telling her he was one of them. "You're so naïve you're dangerous."

Amo checked the *Times* shot critically. Good smile and head angle, arm looked strained. Could've shot more light on the body to pick up the scales. She pointed to the *Times* ad, a full page of Amo in a mermaid's tail. "That's me," she said and patted her chest, palmed the ad, frowned, and sighed.

Mal said, "You don't relate to it?"

"I was trying to feel the glamour, but you can't from inside." Amo shrugged.

"Use it for an ego trip, dummy."

"Maybe a side trip." Amo loved nakedness, hated dirtiness, as she did in her writing. But too much depended on *their* reaction. When she posed nude for the menu cover of the Dutch Treat Club, the publishers thought she was amusing. Then she posed for an amateur who wanted to tie her hands over a beam and shoot her swinging. (She left fast.) She hated modeling for amateurs but she needed their money to survive. One thing about hating modeling, she didn't have to hate writing. Modeling composed her fears and fantasies neatly.

"I wish I *did* look like that," Amo said wistfully. She knew how much makeup she wore, how much retouching was done, how the lighting carefully hid her defects. Amo felt inferior to her image.

"You know when I'll feel beautiful, Mal?" She brushed against his shoulder. "When the book is done."

"I know, babe."

Chapter 10
Show Biz

All over New York everybody sat alone with a lover, a fleeting romance, sipping a drink in the pad before going out Saturday night. All over town they turned on the music—in this case, a portable hi-fi given Amo by an admiring amateur after the second robbery—and discussed life as they knew it. W.R. had given Amo permission to propose to Malachi, seeming both put out and non-committal about it.

Into the low roar of the Five Spot, the musicians' and writers' ethnic pub, Amo called it. She clutched with various writers blustering at the bar—Truman Capote surrounded by his fans, Allen Ginsberg surrounded by orbiting poets, and several pale editors. All surpassed their images in paunch. Rexroth was reading and Larry Rivers was sitting in with Mingus—an event. They sat at a table for two in the dark urban forest beneath a pinpoint lamp.

Sipping bad Chablis, Amo inspected the other men. They looked handsomer than Malachi. Why didn't she know them, why were they with other women? That one talking to Capote—God, those eyes. He looked

like he could lay her essence in midair. She pretended
to be with him and from that vantage point inspected
Mal. As an unknown, Mal was devastating—so he was
okay; he photographed okay. No families in the joint,
no children, nobody looked married. Everybody gazed
insatiably at everyone else, hungry-orbed New York-
ers.

They couldn't hear Rexroth's poetry through the
jazz. Everybody clapped wildly and the important
people drifted away, leaving the place cozy.

After today's ordeal, Amo decided to plunge right
into her proposal, no holds barred. How could she
keep wading through this hogshit? "Mal—?"

"How'd you like me to call you Ah—?"

"But Malachi is so formal."

"Amo's so freaky."

"Ah don't think so."

"Ah do."

"You're suffering from upward mobility symp-
toms," said Amo. "I'm going to call you Moe."

They fell about laughing, Mal reaching under the
table and up her thigh. "She's my front-page filly—my
moo-moo-moooovie star," Malachi wound on.

Amo sat back. How to propose through all this
scurrying wit? "Why don't you just say I love you?"
She jabbed him.

Malachi jumped.

The waiter appeared, imperious. They ordered more
wine and club sandwiches, fast. Waiter departed.

Amo eyed Mal, dead level.

"Because I don't know what love is. Who does these

days? Why pretend, why lie?" Mal sat back, patting his straggly hair, jaw tensing.

"Affection, tenderness, lust, like-mindedness, that's what it is," Amo said angrily. "Need, closeness, temperamental affinity."

"You can feel all those things without love, Amo."

"How?"

His expansive face looked distinctly unpleasant, as if he'd swallowed something awful. "Not everyone believes in politics. Not everyone believes in love. Besides, I'd rather fuck you."

Wine clinked down as they sat silent.

At the next table a beard huddled with a blonde said, "I had to break if off—it was getting serious." She nodded. "Who wants to get involved?"

Amo spewed out her Chablis and gurgled with laughter. "I'll never beat this rap."

Mal brightened instantly. "Did I show you the latest review?" He handed her a page torn from the *Village Voice* that mentioned "an enterprising performance by mobile-faced Malachi Stein in *Dirty Is Better*."

"Fantastic, love. Be sure and take it to the Reading."

"Fear not."

She took his hands. "I hope it runs."

"Yeah— Speaking of dirt, what's new with your lecherous fans?"

Amo's body tensed. Why tell him a sick story that would only amuse him? "Do you think I should have contempt for men because they're all out for the same thing basically?"

"What?"

"That's what the hotshot producers said today who wanted me to perform for them." At A.M.C., a big movie agency, she was shuffled off to two producers who wanted a fast body to do some simple routine on their new TV show. On Go-Sees, Amo always showed her short story in *Partisan Review*, as well as the *Meat* centerfold, and the anthology with her story in it. She wanted them to know she was not just a body, that she had a functioning brain. She was proud of her little publications. Also they saw ten to forty girls for each job and she hoped it would help them remember her. On the back of her composites she wrote Model & Writer.

The two producers were not interested. They interviewed her as if she were a dunce to see if she had poise, made her walk for them, criticized her hair and makeup, and said she didn't know how to handle herself on a Go-See. "I didn't flirt enough, they said; I was too businesslike. Apparently I didn't understand it was a sexual competition for jobs, and if I wanted to be noticed among all the gorgeous flesh, I had to spread my legs."

Mal jumped.

"Actually. As I waited for the Man in the reception room, holding my modeling portfolio on my knees, I should slowly but subtly let my legs come apart. It wouldn't work unless I wore black panties, they said, to entice the Man and make him think he was really seeing something. But of course he wouldn't be. They'd show me, they said, how simple it was. They sat me down on a chair then settled themselves directly across the paneled room to instruct me, very businesslike.

"I sat there with my portfolio open on my locked knees, thinking of the years of effort that took—muscles forming to close legs—when I'd do better as a slut."

"The point is," said the alcoholic WASP lobster, "the Man's got to think it's accidental, that you're unaware of it." "Yeh, he don't want to be conned," put in the tubby Jew, "like a job's being done on him." Amo frowned; they seemed so serious. "Go ahead now, we'll see how you do."

Amo tried and nothing happened. "He thinks you're a cunt"—the fat Jew waved his arm—"so what're ya gonna do about it—ya got to use him." The WASP drunk uncrossed his brittle arms, "Or you won't get anywhere in *this* game." They both leaned forward, elbows on knees, "Go on, now."

Amo tried to part her legs. "No guts," said the slob. "She'll always be a sucker." Amo tried till tears came to her eyes. "She doesn't want to be in show biz," said the juicer. Like maniacs, they stared at the point between her knees.

Suddenly Amo screamed, *"You're* conning me—you're doing a *job* on me. I'll tell you who I have contempt for—bastards like you! You ought to see your faces right now, you animated turds." She roared out, slamming inner sanctum doors. "How can you work for such shits?" she yelled at the shocked secretary.

Malachi's face didn't quite reflect Amo's feelings.

When she finished, she stared at him skeptically. "Did that turn you on?"

"Some way to get your jollies," he said politely. He took her hands, squeezed, eyes bright.

Amo was beginning to feel Used as a model, as a woman.

Amo slept with anyone she wanted and nobody she didn't want. She never slept with photographers or agency moguls to get jobs and she lost lots of big money jobs that way. The big shootings in the Islands, the TV shows, and big-time TV commercials went to the models who'd make it fun for the boys. Amo wasn't going to be a whore just because it paid. It meant that many of her Go-Sees were a total waste.

Sometime later Jack Carter sent her to see Teddie Shields, the head of M.T.M.C., about a TV show. Amo showed him her humble stories and photos. He came out from behind his huge polished desk, smiled brightly as if he didn't see her, and tried to feel her breasts.

The juicer was right. Show biz was too dirty for Amo.

Chapter 11
Puff, Puff

"Come on, Amo, you know I don't relax except at the studio."

"Give it a whirl, Commissar."

Immediately Mal thrust his chin out and his mouth drew down into a self-involved pout. Amo marveled at the sheer droop of his pout but this time they went to her place. She propelled him along like a reluctant bull being teased to market, popping his rear now and then.

"This dump stinks," he offered as she unlocked the entrance.

"Yes, pity the poor lass," she laughed.

In the kitchen she uncovered the joints in the Kent pack in the box of soapsuds. When she came out, Mal was stretched out naked among the dime-store pillows on the swooping double bed, brown eyes flashing open self-love, black brows emphasizing ever greater degrees of enthusiasm as he shook his cock at her.

"Wittgenstein, you have no sense of timing." She dragged on the joint and passed it to him, sucking hard, mouth like a celestial choir chanting "O—O—O."

Tonight Amo was so tight Malachi could almost

hear the drumbeats sending warnings from one part of her body to another. "Why don't you walk around and pose for me a little, without the bra and pantihose?"

"Goddamn it, Mal,"—she turned up the volume,—"I'm trying to propose to you."

"On second thought,"—hands behind head— "leave the bra on and put on a garter belt and hose. Tapped cooz—beats pantihose any day."

"Mal,"—she held his knees—"we've been going together for almost two years, and I want to . . . live together." She tried to force love through his pornographic eyes.

That stopped him, momentarily. "Another Love & Marriage Seizure,"—he checked his watch—"right on time—every six months." He put on the Irish. "If I just roll with the punches, from growling one minute, she'll be giggling."

"*Stop it,*" she demanded with that deep resonance that frightens men. "Can't you respect the possibility?"

Mal grinned, dismayed at her, pouted and pulled in his chin. "Marriage is not for me, love, you know that."

Amo's face glowed dangerously tight, as if the fire within were consuming her. "I didn't *say* marriage, but *closeness.* Casual, no strings. . . ."

"Vhat can I say?" Mal lifted his arms like a comedian conning the audience after a bad joke. "Vhat, tell me?"

Tears rimmed her eyelids, like lost moon slivers. "The twentieth century again?"

"The twenty-first Amo, that's where we're at in *this*

city. We already have the population explosion—we
live in boxes. We've already lost nature, and individu-
ality, and love." Such things brought out his real
passion and he looked infinitely lovable.

"Bullshit, I'm unique and so are you. More
brand-new folks are born every day. We'll soon take
over Earth." By which she meant it was all according
to who looked at what, and how.

Mal dabbed at her eyes with the pillowcase. "You're
a sensualist, Amo. I'm a politician—much more
dependable. If a sensualist falls for you, it's sheer luck
your number came up."

"Bullshit. A sensualist is a politician with emotions." She grappled to engage his eyes in a real
contact and felt surrounded by crowds, felt like one of
the audience.

Mal spoke light, soothingly. "Who do most people
marry? They marry the image of torture they knew
from their parents. You wouldn't want me to do that to
you, would you, Amo?"

"Like so many things you say,"—she looked at him
wearily—"it doesn't apply. My parents aren't from
here."

"Maruvia again?" His eyes almost crossed with
consternation.

"Never mind. I only had my mother, the Judge."

"Hey, great! Pose for me like you wouldn't for
them." He pushed up her skirt and tugged at her
underclothes.

"What?"

"Sit across from me without your panties, with your
legs apart."

He scratched her, yanking at the panties, and she slapped him across the face. "You fucking automoton!"

His mouth sucked in like a lemon, his face whitened to a slab. "Stop that,"—he grabbed her wrists—"or I'll have to take the whip to you—not gently or playfully."

She twisted but he wouldn't let her hands free.

"You know I don't like violence unless it's a game," he threatened.

When her hands got slippery enough, she jerked them away. "I'm tired of your dirty little games. I want something *real*."

"Real blows, real pain." His eyes glinted with tender remembrance. "I once knew a girl who really enjoyed whipping. I'd beat her till she came, shining with sweat and oozing." His mouth jerked with weak viciousness; he licked his lips. Then he winked and yawped with laughter.

"Did they put her away?"

"For awhile."

"Real blows, real crud—Mal, horror is not the only thing real. There's real . . . love. I *know*."

He stopped up his ears, tried to make his eyes laugh.

"Go on, leave—you fucking sadistic hebe priest. *Get out!*"

Mal got up. "I'll fix us a drink."

She pushed at his back, the small blonde figure. "Get out of my pad before I call the fuzz."

"Oh ho ho," he doubled over chuckling and loped off to the kitchen.

Tears filmed Amo's eyes. She went into the bathroom to call W.R., who came in reluctantly.

W.R.: "You know I'm not amused by these clandestine calls in the midst, so to speak."

AMO (surprised): "You're jealous."

W.R. (miffed): "Why must you operate with *me* on Earth level?"

AMO: "W.R., why won't anybody marry me? Or live with me? He's not the first."

W.R.: "You know why. The exploitative system down there—you don't really fit into it. We didn't program you for marriage. In fact, we're rather disappointed—"

AMO: "I'm *alone*, W.R. I write alone. I model with a couple of people then come back here, alone. I *live* alone—except when I'm with him Saturday night and Sunday morning."

W.R: "It's true, you don't have the Interconsciousness System down there."

AMO: "Since I have it and they don't, what can I do but seek the physical bond? For company."

W.R.: "But you must know you are over-qualified for marriage. He considers you too superior to be a wife, unless normalized by money or fame. Superior women are acceptable there if they offer this sort of dowry as apology. Also you don't possess those menial second-rate female characteristics he craves."

AMO: "He *seems* to accept me."

W.R.: "Yes, but you don't puff him enough. He's unable to feel those second-rate male characteristics he identifies with at this primitive stage. Once we get you famous, it'll all go easier for you."

AMO: "W.R., you're such a dreamer."

W.R.: "Besides, you don't want to marry him, A.M.O. You want to get rid of him."

AMO: "Really, W.R.!"

Mal tapped on the bathroom door. "Who're you talking to?"

Amo emerged, took the drink he handed her, and said, "My Wrist Radar, who else?"

"Yes, well, I'm so glad I asked." His look of patient disgust intersected with hers of steadfast dominion.

"Malachi, how can Earthmen desire me passionately and not want to marry me?"

With that, he slouched comfortably again. "Your best characteristic, Amo. You don't know how to make a man feel guilty. Most women know it in their bones."

"The feminine wiles again?"

"Yeah, babe. You can't do a number on me after two years. You got to work a man from the very beginning. A man looks at you and he knows you don't want a strong shoulder, you want a strong cock. A man would have a hard time believing you needed him to prop you up."

This always confused Amo. "But I don't *want* anyone to prop me up."

"You see? Most men have weak cocks so they pretend to have strong shoulders." His eyes danced. He loved to explain things.

"But not you?" she said.

Mal looked desperate. "You're just not my idea of a wife." He cackled, "Like who wants to marry a spaced-out chick from Maruvia?" Now he had it to use.

"I'm just an ordinary woman," she lied, pleaded. "I want a man of my own. Maybe I even want to have children." Her eyes widened with the novelty of this thought. "I want to be *with* a man, part of ordinary life. Instead I'm up to my ass in tinsel and sex tricks."

"I'm so sorry," he huffed. He began pacing, naked, heavy-footed.

"I'm sorry too," she said sadly.

To Amo, he suddenly seemed helpless before her onslaught of emotion, biding his time, suspended. She sighed, enveloped with monstrous Maruvian sympathy. You can't blame a person for not being what they cannot, for not being you. His hair silkened, his chest loomed, his muscular thighs hypnotized her: all this time he'd been there naked and she hadn't even noticed. "Let's . . . forget it, angel." She stretched up to him, her form following his, and embraced him.

Mal kissed her in his passionate overmoist manner, lips like a great dribbling baby's, that always turned her instantly off then totally on, by transforming her being. Amo was fond of transformation from one state to another. Mal could do it, the writing, even the modeling, the light in the air. Suddenly she stung with desire, pounded with molten lava under the skin, a raging interior heat with nothing but the stoker in mind.

She reached for his ballooning swell but it had been punctured and sagged. "With a little help?" She waggled it and sucked, caressing the cool balls with her face.

"Sorry, love,"—Mal removed her face—"the idea of marriage made me lose my hard-on."

They went to bed. In that hour of cowering vulnerability before dawn, Amo woke up bawling, gasping, and screaming like a two-year-old. She'd lost again, she always lost, and she didn't know what was wrong with her. Enough within sleep to permit herself, she roiled and raved like a person being flayed.

In the morning Malachi had an early appointment. "Next time you have a seizure," said the oracle, "remember this—one good fuck is worth a thousand words." He went off to the shower.

Amo sat up in bed, hands behind her head, deciding. When he bussed her good-bye she said, "Don't bother to come back or phone, Mal."

She spoke so quietly he just laughed.

Chapter 12
The Great Minor Celebrity

Aphrodite the Stripper got up from her rejection by Mal to go make a living as a heroine. They greeted her at the train, her real fans, the silent overstuffed daddies of the world.

Don, the seedy officious President of the Camden Camera Club, stepped forward. He was backed by several bears of engineers, a kindly old master watchmaker, a sunny cynical Irish cop, a gray accountant, a couple of splashy salesmen, and four electronics technicians. A mixed bag of blue and white collar, they were all dedicated to the Art of the Camera. They shot nudes to Be Creative. They vied in telling Amo how many of her pictures they'd collected from various magazines, as she resisted being their alabaster idol.

"Yeah, Don," said Darrell the fuzz, "I know one ya missed—four-page spread on Amo by Alex Heish in *Modern Photography*."

"This month, Darrell?" frowned Don, outdone.

"I missed it too," Amo laughed.

"Yeah, the issue on the stands now. I'll mail you three-four copies, okay, Amo?"

"Swell. I'll tell Alex. He didn't know when it was scheduled."

"I still think your *Meat* layout tops 'em all," Bob the bland engineer declared himself.

Two of the technicians shambled over. "Amo, would you mind signing these?" They handed her several eight-by-ten color prints from the last session at the clubhouse in Camden.

"Hey! They're great," she knew to say. She autographed them—"Besos, Amo Coove."

They drove to the Pennsylvania woods.

High forest parts to reveal glistening white maiden on rock precarious in midst of gushing stream. Ten clothed gentlemen on one bank and six on other bank lift, in unison, box hung on groins and click it at her. Click, clickety click. Manet's *Picnic on the Grass*, Amo was thinking.

"Hey, Amo, where ya hiding that sweet smile?" called Sal the salesman.

"This is my classic ballet face, Sal." Amo had been doing pure form poses, face serious.

"Ya look grumpy to me," the kindly old master watchmaker offered.

Too straightforward—where was the coy shrinking attempt to please? Modeling was like a penance to be tolerated in the interest of art. As if she had to expose her bare body to the elements, like St. Simeon Stylites, and what was more—not complain. Show patience, not chagrin. A warm tolerance, not irritation. Do not hate those who devour you with their eyes: love. And by turning hate to love, make your face beautiful beyond their power to desecrate it.

Amo knew what they wanted. She slung her arms and tits into the air and whipped out the big grin with the big pearlies asparkle, ready to bite, and the boys came to with a jolt. Well . . . poor guys; if they had any taste, they'd shoot flowers and faces and ghettos, and she'd starve.

"Amo, I can tell you love your work," said Don. "You're so natural."

"How's my worshipful sexpot, better now?" Mal was on the phone.

"Umm."

"Living the fantasy life of the everyday housewife, and dreaming of marriage like a kid." He was at the top of his form. "Would she howl you down, the housewife, I mean." Mal was convinced he could give Amo what she wanted: the opposite of what she claimed to want. It didn't occur to him that she might actually know her own mind.

"Ah, yes . . . unlimited sexual and intellectual adventure," Amo said sardonically. "Continuation is inevitable."

"Be over about nine," he said.

"No. No more. Finished," she said expressionlessly.

"I'll call you tomorrow," he said casually.

"Listen to me, Mal," Amo said in Maruvian tones, "I

have the same right to say No as you do. If you deny me in a greater sense, I don't have to accept you in a smaller."

"Out of nowhere, Amo—what *is* this?"

"Mal, I want to find a man to be *with*. I'm tired of being your wet dream."

Requisite moments of silence before Mal said tightly, "You're making me very very angry."

"Then I'll hang up," and she did.

Perhaps fifteen dramatic versions of this encounter were staged over the phone in the next week. One night the downstairs buzzer buzzed relentlessly and knowing it was Mal, Amo didn't answer. But somebody rang him into the building and soon he was pounding on her door.

"I see your feet under the door. Goddamn it, open up!" he bellowed.

"Not when you're in that insane mood."

Mal heaved his shoulder against the door, determined to push it in. Crash—and the door shuddered. Crunch—it creaked and groaned. Amo listened for sounds of neighbors emerging from their apartments to pull him away and save her. Silence.

"Mal, I'm calling the police," she warned.

"You would do that,"—he creamed the door in a frenzy—"and get it on my record."

"You'd break in and hurt me—I'd protect myself." She went to the phone and stood there, holding the receiver.

The downstairs buzzer rang again and she answered it.

"Police! We're coming up," echoed heavy voices and treads from below.

Mal, silenced, then whispered for help. "What'll I do?"

Amo whispered back, "Go into the hall bathroom and lock it from the inside and I'll say you ran out of the building." The bathroom was for the two single rooms on each floor.

Two burly blues stomped to Amo's door. "Where is he? We got a call."

"Thank God you're here," Amo sighed theatrically. "He ran out—not two minutes ago. But look at the damage to this door!"

"Mind if we search?"

"Of course not." The soul of generosity.

They moseyed about Amo's apartment then walked out into the hall and tapped on the bathroom door.

The fuzz who tapped called in, "You lucked out this time, buddy. The lady don't want to charge you."

They gave Amo a weary disgusted eye and left the building. Amo instantly locked her door. Mal must have quietly left. They did not exchange another word.

Chapter 13
Time Stopping Pill

At Venus' Rental Studio, Amo posed pinup and nude for an amateur who was a paraplegic. He sat chopped off in a wheelchair, no older than Amo, wearing service medals from Vietnam on his sport shirt. As he wheeled out, slowly clanking, a priest walked in, Boston-ruddy and jolly. His model didn't show, so Amo posed for Father Maclarney as well, pinup and nude.

After the session he put an arm around her and tried to snuggle up.

"Your profession doesn't permit that," said Amo, "and neither does mine."

In the downstairs hall of the Dear Old Dump, Amo picked her hot mail off the radiator and went upstairs to her pad, where her own radiator hammered out a greeting. "Hello, old tool." She patted it. The floor creaked like old bones and the icebox moaned about breaking down again. Hanging on the closet door was the big Mexican straw bag for Fire Drills. Amo mentally practiced tossing all her writing in the bag and heading out the door, coat on, cash in pocket.

Instantly the phone rang.

"This Amo Coove, the model?"

"This is she." Amo had finally learned to use a cool business voice.

"Ya know what I'm gonna do f'ya?"

"Who's calling, please?"

"I'm gonna fuck ya till ya cream all over me. I'm gonna fuu—uuu—uuuck ya. . . ."

Amo put the receiver down on its side and let him squawk at himself while she opened her mail. She'd also learned no response was the best response, and much easier on her, and that if she hung up right away, he'd call back three-four times.

There was a small package containing sheer bikini panties. Stapled inside the crotch was part payment of $30 cash and a business card with a note: "Wish I was here. See you Tuesday at 7:00 P.M. Love, Fulton." Fulton and his playpen erotica. "Tsk, tsk, you're a bad boy, Fulton," she'd say to him Tuesday and he'd blush adoringly, shoot her for two hours, and never lay a hand on her.

There was an envelope from Shiver Photo with an eight-by-ten black-and-white of Amo in bikini and yachtsman's cap with a note that it would be in the New York *Times* next Sunday to advertise the Boat Show opening at the Coliseum. There was a thick envelope from *Meat* with two copies of next month's issue enclosed. *Tidbit Review,* the cover proclaimed the presence of the past three years' Tids inside. Amo opened it to a nude of herself that she liked better than the one they'd used before. She remembered the phone, listened to the man breathe, hung up gingerly.

A rather dirty envelope contained a six-page missive in green ink from Rod. Rod told her how "our thighs will flow together in eternal harmony" and that he felt confident his "prowess would be satisfactory to your utmost desires and cravings." Poor Rod. Then there was a brief note from her Earthmother, who was the only woman trial judge in the Atlanta Municipal Courts system. After many years of being rejected for her strength, Amo's Earthmother had given up and was now living with a lesbian professor; she had to relate to somebody.

Amo began her mental flipflop toward an evening of writing with forty-five minutes of exercise while dinner cooked. She stripped down to bra and panties and warmed up, as in spatial ballet.

The phone rang. Some agent asked if she'd like to go on a blind date with Buntington Burford. "Already have," she said, "he's a dunce." The agent laughed. Olaf Cattifi had asked her to join his harem. She'd get free clothes and go out with him now and then and, who knows, she might end up on top of the list. "Everything's not for sale," she'd said, and he seemed surprised. A rapacious crew, these monied tail chasers. Well, one thing about sleeping with Pelf—she didn't have to wonder what it was like, as the rest of the world did.

She stretched out on the floor on the old bedspread for the leg-ups and -outs. The eternal phone rang again. It was Pierre Schlesinger wondering if she'd go out with him, the ex-governors of North Carolina and Florida, and their wives.

Amo was tempted. "No, sorry, I work at night during the week."

"But it's just one night."

"It's always just one night."

"But you can make it up tomorrow morning."

Amo's eyes teared. "I wouldn't write at night if I didn't have to make a living in the daytime." Feeling deprived, she got angry. "I'm sorry, Pierre, I've got to hang up."

Amo raged through her exercises and sat down to her solitary dinner. She was rereading Dostoyevsky's *Notes from Underground.* She thrilled to it like music—the subtleties, the interplays, ironies springing like human shapes from the ominous flow of words. She yearned, ached, to be able to do that. She'd give her left arm—she was left-handed—to be Dostoyevsky. She'd give her life, both here on Earth and on Maruvia. Yes! she'd be willing to be almost a century dead to be Dostoyevsky. She thought herself back to his day and into his bones and walked with him over a bridge and along a park in St. Petersburg. Burning with genius. Like Amo, playing an outcast for the master, horrified by society, enraged with herself.

Amo fixed coffee, cleaned the desk, read over notes and bits of the previous chapter, stared out the window, gave up in despair and got to work. The novel, presumably autobiographical, was about her previous life on Maruvia, where she'd lived thirty years (aging only fifteen) before being sent down here as a fifteen-year-old girl in an Atlanta orphanage. Her Earthmother, who was divorced and lonely, had found her there.

Amo had been one of the first to take the Time Stopping Pill when it was finally perfected for Maruvians over the age of ten. So she had retained extreme youth but acquired enough Transcendence to handle Earth Mission #309, it was hoped. Transcendence was the Maruvian aptitude for entering into another state, into the conditions of other planets or solar systems. W.R. always claimed an Earth mission was descendence but he was kidding, wasn't he?

Most Maruvians were now taking the Time Stopping Pill around age twenty which, of course, meant they wouldn't accept an Earth mission. Once you hit Earth, you started aging normally again like Earthlings. But Amo was a "hopeless moralist" (W.R. speaking) who thought she could succeed where others had failed.

When she learned that Earthmen still suffered the Gobbling Deficiency, Amo volunteered. Her book would tell them how it had been cured on Maruvia. The Gobbling Deficiency, sometimes called the killer instinct, was that maudlin aggressiveness that concerned itself with power first and people second. That was why Amo had small belief in Earth politics: it was all power and competition, based on fear and spurious face-saving moralities. Though she wanted to believe that didn't apply to Malachi. She'd wanted very much to believe it.

The book started with Amo's first memories—of seeing her father pregnant. She had opened her unborn eyes, and beyond the gadgetry and the plastic bubble, there was her father smiling down. The clear plastic bubble containing the incubator was attached to his stomach. All the gadgetry was brightly painted so he could proudly explain the mechanism to his friends. Some of the men wore a skinlike foam covering over their bubble to simulate a condition of Not Knowing, but not her ebullient father. More men were having babies than women, a novelty expected to wear off though W.R. reported they were still hooked on the process. Maruvian women were amused and relieved, since they were so involved in reforming the planet.

Amo wrote about the problems the Time Stopping Pill had caused before it was perfected for those over age ten. As a child she remembered hearing her Aunt Xiir and another lady talking in the park. Aunt Xiir held her older cousin in her arms, whom she'd had the old way the year before Bubble Birth.

"Hello, there. How's your baby?"

"Oh, fine." Aunt Xiir bounced the baby wearily.

"How old is she now?"

"She's twenty-two—total."

"Nice."

"We've decided to let her start growing this year."

"Oh?"

"Yes. I had her when I was twenty-one. We think it's time to stop waiting for that damn Over-Ten Pill. After all, I'm—uh—forty-three now. I'll be sixty by the time she's a young swinging chick. Now at sixty, who can be jealous of a gorgeous blooming daughter?"

"Hmm," said the other doubtfully.

"How's your brood?"

"Fine, fine. We stopped them all at ten, if you remember."

"Yes, I hope it won't be a problem for you. They say the planet has more ten-year-olds than any other age these days." Amo's mother hadn't stopped her growth at all, hoping for perfection of the Over-Ten Pill.

"Bound to happen," said Xiir's friend. "But we've worked out a unique growing plan. Upon our deaths or when we're sixty—whichever comes first—they start growing and as our complete beneficiaries. The insurance people thought it was brilliant spacing."

"Indeed, it is. By then they may have perfected the Pill for people of twenty—wouldn't that be nice?—or somewhat above ten anyway. Not that it's going to do *us* much good."

"No." Sigh. "It's really not fair, is it?"

"No." Xiir switched the baby to the other hip. "But maybe by then, being ten will be all the rage."

"I'm old-fashioned, I guess. I'll always prefer twenty—"

"Or even thirty, if people had any taste these days, which they don't."

"Sad to say."

"I must run. My best to Zag."

"My best to Thon." Poor Aunt Xiir missed Bubble Birth and the Over-Ten Pill. Timing is all.

Even on Maruvia, people were deprived till the Pill was perfected for those over ten, and virtual ageless-ness was attained. Amo was fourteen when it happened and she took it at fifteen. Only heroes did something that might jeopardize such a blissful way of life, and they were honored on Maruvia. Your common Maruvian, however, was totally addicted to eternal youth. They ran down internally but at a much slower rate. The important thing was that it didn't show. Nobody had to look at it. Kids who wanted to win the charm game took it at fifteen and ten. Finally, to restore equality and standards to the beauty game, a law was passed that no one could take the Time Stopping Pill under age eighteen.

The Time Stopping Pill was almost the final equalizer. When they took the TSP at eighteen, it freed Maruvians from the need for security because they'd always be desirable. Mono Love, Couple Love vanished in the daily unendurable sense. Amo's mother and father visited each other but didn't live together. Amo visited both but lived with the other kids in the kid garden. Amo's mother helped to prove the existence of the Gobbling Deficiency which led, of course, to the vote to cure it. *That* was the final equalizer.

Dreams of glory streaming down on Amo at four A.M. in her one-room dump in the dark city, writing her first novel. Like many another, Amo suffered the Great American Novel delusion that art is transcendence and transcendence life. The daily struggle with her imagination offered surcease, and ever greater solitude.

She was banging away at four A.M. when the phone rang. Wondering who was smashed or suicidal, she picked it up.

It was Malachi. He wanted to come by. Almost a year had passed since the breakup, a year of hard work, many men, no love.

"It's too late, Mal. Besides, I'm working."

But he could hear the excitement in her voice. "I

waited till now so I wouldn't interrupt your work," he said.

Amo's voice wobbled, lilted. "Come on over, you lying sniggling bastard."

"I'll give you till four thirty, okay?"

"Marvelous." Amo's rationale had crumbled with the endless impact of loneliness. It was not the setup but the man that mattered.

W.R. signaled Amo in an almost panic-stricken way, again and again, but she ignored the call. At a moment like this, W.R. sounded like just so much static.

Elated, Amo wrote about the general astonishment when it was discovered that 65 to 75 percent of Maruvian men suffered the Gobbling Deficiency. The planet was tired of their wars. Finally they had killed each other to the point where there were a third more women than men. With the help of the sympathetic men, Maruvia voted to program it out. A new process was developed by one of the leading women scientists to implant female hormones in deficient fetuses. The adult male populace was injected through the water supply.

W.R. kept buzzing.

"Cool it, W.R.," Amo said without bothering to answer.

The picture of Malachi went back up on the dresser. There he was, slouched in jeans, chest bare except for beads, eyes glinting, hair intense. Now that he was on his way, the long months without him seemed to ache in her bones. As if an intolerable pain finally surfaced now that it could be ejected.

Chapter 14
The Gobbling Deficiency

Two hours later Malachi arrived, didn't kiss her, posed leaning against the door in leather pants and fringes, hair longer and blacker, face almost wolfish, lines from weight loss under his eyes and souring his mouth.

Amo embraced him, felt him hold back. He sent out waves of suffering that flooded her heart with intense Maruvian sympathy.

"How's the acting?" she asked. "Didn't I see a credit several months ago?"

"No, you did not," he interrupted. "I haven't had an acting job since Dirty folded."

"I'm sorry."

"Still shooting asshole ads for the occasional third-rate client."

She took his hands, which he let her have, limp. "I'm so sorry."

"How's your work?" he asked brusquely, eyes seeming pinpointed and distracted at once.

"I'm really into the book . . . it's almost a pleasure. Modeling—I suppose it's the same, only I hate it more.

All those pig-eyed people who want to tear into my flesh, only the law won't allow it so they chew me with their eyes."

His lip curled then his face opened out. "Still turning them phrases, eh, kid?"

When Malachi smiled, the moon walked the walls and nudged them to the bed. Amo was ecstatic; she didn't care what the arrangements were, if they could be together. They hung their clothes on the floor and fell on the bed. They made love in that way that melts muscle and bone, turns nerves to honey, floats bodies like feathers from a weightless center bathed in clinging juices. So it seemed to Amo. Then Mal pulled out and told her to scoot to the edge of the bed. Kneeling, he went down on her, with his marauding fountain of a mouth.

Suddenly she felt something tugging at her ankle and when she tried to move her foot, she couldn't. She flexed her ankle again. It seemed to be tied.

Amo sat up on her elbows. "What in hell are you up to?" Her right ankle was clearly tied by a rope to the foot of the bed.

"Be still while I do the other one," Mal said, eyes twinkling.

"Why Mal?" She stared in disbelief.

"It's erotic." He was now licking her toes. "Doesn't my demented Tidbit like to be taken?"

"Have I ever indicated that I do?" Her foot yanked at the rope. "Ow! Undo this thing."

"Can't you ever do anything for me?" He licked the sole of her foot and up around her ankle. "Just because I want you to?"

"It makes me feel so helpless. I don't like to be helpless."

"But that's the idea, that's the game." He leaned his head on her leg, kissed her up to the center, opened her like a pear, and stuck his tongue in everywhere. "Please? You know I won't hurt you, baby. . . ."

Amo was so hot, her foot so wet, that she hardly knew he had the other one tied till he'd finished doing it.

"Now, that's not so bad, is it?" Mal tickled her feet and licked them till she laughed.

"Come here." She wanted him inside her again. He slid slowly in, at the same time diving for her left breast as if he were going to bite it off, laughing when she jerked away and said, "Don't." He did the same to the right, she didn't flinch, and he landed a bit too hard. "That hurts," she said. "No, it doesn't," he said and pulled his head back to show her the amazing length of nipple he'd grown. She was steaming, tensing, rising, ready to shoot, when he pulled out and tried to force his way into the back.

Amo hollered, shifting away. "You know I can't take more than a finger there." It ached like a blow, like brass knuckles to the soft part of the arm.

"Oh yes, you can if you relax. You just don't want to." He held her down with his body and nudged at the opening, which was tightly closed.

Amo shifted her hips again. "Mal, we tried. You know I can't." She pulled at her tied feet, heart jumping. "Please!"

Amo had only her arms free. He pinned her arms

and laid his head on her breasts. "If you don't stop squirming, I'm going to really bite," said Mal. But Amo couldn't be still because every time he dented the area, it felt like a hot poker and her hips leaped away. Mal clamped his teeth onto her breast and she screamed with the pain.

"Shut up," he said, and hit her across the face. She raised up to bite his chest and he slammed her down. He punched her again and again, whipping her head from side to side, his face insanely calm. "You're just another one of these cunts that's ruined my life," he snarled.

Amo knew instinctively the harder she resisted, the harder she'd be hit. "Please, please. . . ."

"That's it, you cunt. Beg me to spare you." He hit her on the breast this time. "That beautiful saleable body—"

Amo tried to twist away, couldn't move. "What are you doing?" She tried to talk sense. "Are you high?"

"You're a cunt, aren't you?" Slam. "Nothing but a lousy cunt."

She was afraid he'd smash a cheekbone or a breast.

"Say it!"

"I'm—"

"A foul stinking cunt. Say it!"

"A stinking cunt. Please. . . . "

Mal's fists flew like a madman with a punching bag. "Take that for good measure—and that—and that."

Amo felt herself turning to mush, then a new fierce pain. Mal bit her stomach till he drew blood. Abruptly he got up, threw his clothes on and went to the door.

"If you call the pigs, I'll have somebody come here and take care of you." He slammed the door and was gone.

Amo wept in horror and disappointment that this could be Mal. She felt smashed, felt as small as he tried to make her feel. A foul stinking cunt. She couldn't wiggle her feet free. The rope cut deeper, her ankles bled. The pain in her breasts and rectum frightened her terribly. She couldn't feel her face at all.

W.R. signaled her again and again but Amo had passed out from the pain.

The next noon the phone rang and rang. It was Pierre Schlesinger. "I just wanted to tell you," he said with great good humor, "what you missed. We ended up at the Carlton with Senator Kennedy."

Chapter 15
Skin

W.R.: "You called the police?"
AMO: "No."
W.R.: "You called a doctor?"
AMO: "No."
W.R.: "Why?"
AMO: "I'm ashamed to have anybody see me—so banged up."
W.R.: "Nonsense!"
AMO: "I feel like an insect, a squashed bug. I feel humiliated because I couldn't do anything to stop him."
W.R.: "Then you feel exactly the way he wants you to. The victim deserves it because the victim can't protect herself. Therefore, the victim is asking for it."
AMO: "This time I thought about gouging his eyes. But he was in such a rage I was afraid he'd kill me."
W.R.: "He would have. He's dangerous when he doesn't get what he wants."
AMO: "You mean me?"

W.R.: "No."

AMO: "You mean acting jobs?"

W.R.: "Precisely. If he's not getting work, it's your fault."

AMO: "Do you think he was on drugs, W.R.?"

W.R.: "What difference?"

AMO: "Helpless . . . loss of control—"

W.R. (furiously): "You mean you'd forgive somebody for killing you because he shot himself up to make it easier?"

AMO: "I just wonder—"

W.R.: "Did he steal anything?"

AMO (shocked): "Of course not."

W.R. (after a silence): "I tried to warn you. . . . "

AMO: "Who can I trust, W.R., if the man who saved my life tries to kill me?"

W.R.: "I'd advise you to forget the love stuff, A.M.O. You're not qualified to survive it. The combination of your superior qualities and that body we gave you seems to bring out hostility."

AMO: "But, W.R., the isolation—the loneliness. . . . "

W.R.: "You must learn to live without love . . . without suffering."

AMO: "I—I can't. Why did you make me a *woman*, W.R.?"

W.R.: "However you do it, A.M.O., you must learn to lower your Maruvian empathy and expand your ego to match theirs. Learn to live off your ego, as successful Earthmen do."

AMO: "Then I'll want to kill him."

W.R.: "That may be possible."

AMO: "I don't want to become a Speck, a Boston Strangler, a blind egomaniac. . . . "

W.R.: "You want to survive?"

AMO: "I want to come back *there.*"

W.R.: "You have to survive to get here. Phone the police—dial Operator."

AMO: "Thanks."

They didn't get Mal. He skipped town the next day. At Amo's insistence, the cops paid several surprise visits to his studio during the next month, but they never got him.

Cancer got Amo. Amo got cancer, to the gynecologist's surprise as well as her own. It may or may not have had anything to do with the assault by Mal, the gynecologist and the cancer surgeon concluded. It was possible but who could tell, after all.

At any rate, it was cancer of the rectum and she should consider herself fortunate, the doctors said, that she was being checked because of the assault or they never would have caught it so early. Undetected, she would have been dead in two years. Swipe, swat— gone. As for her breasts, the cancer surgeon assured her that he'd do all he could to see that she was able to keep both of them, but there was internal damage— bruises and irritation—that could become malignant at any time, who could tell.

Into the hospital Amo went and came out with a sore rectum from which skin inside the opening had been removed, thereby supposedly removing the neat cancer. The doctor was nice; he let her keep her breasts for now.

Suddenly Amo felt the sharks circling and she alone there in the endless black water. As far as eye could see, only Amo and ocean and circling teeth.

AMO: "What do they want from me, W.R.?"

W.R.: "Your skin—everything you've got, they can make use of."

AMO: "What can I do?"

W.R.: "Swim."

When she finally slept, Amo dreamed a TV show. On camera, twenty-five or so mangled people were lain out in a Flower Power pattern, with clumps of severed limbs and clothes forming the center of the daisy. The announcer came on: "Victims, stay off the streets and stop causing this carnage! Potential victims out after dark are a threat to the community and deserve what they get."

The camera dollied in and showed: old woman (raped first), young woman (raped first), paraplegic vet, draft dodger in prison garb, jailed nun for peace, black maid picked up for prostitution, fourteen-year-old Welfare mother picked up for prostitution, a black junkie, a Puerto Rican pillhead, and a white drunk, an aging stew (thirty) turned secretary, a secretary turned call girl, a fifty-year-old teacher and her nineteen-year-old student lover, a commune that had sat down in the way of a tank, and for sentiment a cocker spaniel named Rover. The announcer was visibly upset over such treatment of poor old Rover.

There was Amo—she found herself—minus breasts and sexual parts. She looked closer—yes, her neck was broken.

Chapter 16
$10,000 at 21

Everybody was awake in Nueva Yorrrk except the free-lancers, the dancers, and the wisps who wash down the skyscrapers at night. At noon the March sky was its usual drugged gray. All over midtown stricken ants tunneled in and out of their towering anthills, covered the streets, and roared about in cabs meeting clients for lunch. Amo to meet a famous editor-in-chief at 21.

Amo had handed the finished novel to her agent and waited for Earth to open. Months passed without tremors. Three publishing houses had the nerve to reject the interplanetary opus. "He wants to offer you $8,000," her agent said, "but don't be too hopeful."

Amo tripped out of the D.O.D. whose entrance was newly decorated with bullet holes, the result of a shoot-out between the fuzz and a fallen member of the force who'd gone berserk in a Broadway bar and killed four civilians. Next door was a gaping hole where a building had burnt out over Christmas. An old type had wished himself such a Merry that his mattress lit up for joy. Amo held Fire Drills more often now.

Seated in the right section of 21 among the right gaudy people, Amo could tell by their enmity they thought she was an old man's darling. The famous editor, Warrington Waver, wore a full head of white hair indented with too small a nose but ponderous cheek and jowl. With his pink skin and horsey jacket and pipe, he reeked of good living.

"That scene where the Earthman beats her"—Waver's eyes lit up—"I can understand why. She was always trying to control things—"

"Like?"

"Her situation with him. Several months ago my wife—I'm married for the fourth time, to a much younger woman—my wife said she wanted to go back for her PhD. I put my foot down." He slammed the table with his fist which shook his jowls and several delicate types nearby.

"Gobble, gobble," said Amo, smiling sweetly. "Then you do agree that the crime usually exceeds the motivation. Most crime does."

"Perhaps. But my thinking is that if he's going to beat her, he'll have to catch her with another man to justify it. Or he wants to leave her and she won't let him—that would do it."

"If I were *your* wife," said Amo, "and I caught you with another woman and beat you, would I be justified?"

"My dear girl, what an insane idea!"

"But that's what you just said." Amo had yet to learn that logic would get her nowhere.

Reddening, Waver huffed and ordered a third martini straight up.

Amo looked about at the painted faces with brilliant hair, expensive wads of fat in Cardin suits, diets in Yves pants. Greedy, wary eyes, out of Francis Bacon and Cuevas, finance and the media, Fifth Avenue and Park.

Waver smiled to himself and said, "What were you like there—on Maruvia?"

"Veeerrrry different. Strong but not aggressive. Kind but not victimized. Creative but not egocentric. Visionary, perhaps. The main thing I remember, that strikes me with wonder, is that I was never tense or anxious."

"No anxiety?"

"No anxiety. Can you imagine?"

He heaved back, smiling. "But that's what gets me up in the morning—anxiety."

Amo laid a sympathetic hand on his arm. "And puts you to bed at night—limpdicked, juiced up, hacking."

Purpling, Waver glared. "See here, young lady."

"Nothing personal," said Amo the overreacher. "An executive malady that results from the Gobbling Deficiency."

"Now that's the only part that turned me off." Waver gripped the table with both hands, leaned his bulk at her. "That men are aggressive to the point of violence," he pounded the table with both fists. "What a silly idea!"

"I didn't originate it," said Amo. "We discovered it, diagnosed it, and treated those in need."

Waver's eyes got canny, his jowls lifted to the ceiling of his familiar kingdom. "We're willing to offer you a $10,000 advance if you'll work with our editors to make your novel more commercial—and if you'll drop this crazy Gobbling Deficiency."

Amo gazed.

"Interested?"

"Sure—"

"Will you make those changes?" His eyes almost laughed.

"You're hurting my feelings," said Amo quietly.

"What's that?"

"You're trying to gobble me up and asking me not to notice the teeth marks."

In the sculpture garden at the Modern, Amo visited Lipschitz' super-*madre*, Lachaise's woman balanced on tiptoe with graceful wobble. She blew it. She felt like a whore. She blew the ten thou. Maybe she could've wheedled and wriggled and won him over—to letting her write what she wanted. No, he'd fox her. Inside the museum, she watched coiffed matrons in perfect pants eyeing long-haired executives in bells trying to pass for artists, who eyed woozy hippie chicks as they gazed sweetly at their fuzzy-haired mates. People, together.

Not like Amo—with no real family. She hadn't seen her Earthmother, the Judge, since she came North five years ago. With no real home. No husband or children. No steady friends or lovers. No steady income. And now, no artistic recognition. Living off the big city parade emotionally as well as for income. So lonely that six people on the MOMA elevator made her feel so gratefully cozy that she smiled at each one. They frowned, looked away. Now that the novel was being rejected, she felt like a whore.

The phone clanged as she unlocked three locks on the Fortress D.O.D. It was the cancer surgeon, who'd been bugging her for months. He was drunk, forty, married, and he wanted to come up. She said no. "I'm going to try to get you to thirty with both your breasts," he mewled, "but you're not giving me much encouragement."

Amo sat in the stocks, her head and arms clamped in stocks, screaming and writhing as the movie camera ground away. Her underclothes were in shreds. The dark basement smelled of rats and urine. She was playing a whore being tortured by her pimp for trying to go it alone. She was the Number One whore, the rebel leader, out to make the girls independent.

"Don't you know what a whore is?" the pimp shouted as her head sagged. "A whore on horse?"

Yes, yes. She was a whore. She deserved it all because she'd failed as a writer.

Upstairs in the living room of the brownstone, they shot her shooting up, she and another whore—a tough girl, an Israeli. Then a blonde med student came up from the basement, throwing up, ketchup smeared on her face. They'd shot a scene of cutting her tongue out. Just girls trying to survive in the Big Apple. It turned out to be a popular movie on Forty-second Street. *Cathouse Rebel*, it was called.

Chapter 17
Benno My Mafia Man

Over the years dozens of men had made Amo offers. A rich movie producer who looked like a penguin wanted her to hostess his East Sixties townhouse. An urbane ad agency president had offered her money and charge accounts at first sight. Trembling, he'd shown her a stack of pinup magazines with her pictures. Sammy Davis wanted her to pose for him but he wouldn't pay the rate; Amo heard he'd paid another model with autographed photos of himself. She double-dated with Jayne Mansfield and she went out with William Gaddis and Rod Serling and Bob Evans. Warren Beatty phoned through Joe Heller when she was in Mexico.

The straightest nude model in town, they said, which meant she didn't put out for jobs, she wasn't kept by anyone, she didn't hustle on the side, she wouldn't pose for open shots or leap out of birthday cakes to be pawed at private parties, she wasn't known on the orgy circuit, she didn't even live with a man, yet she wasn't a lesbian. Over the years Amo acted as if she could make her business respectable simply by insisting on it. When she turned thirty, Amo had been modeling five years.

She was independent, she did an honest day's work and accepted no gratuities, paid nobody with skin. A fool, in other words. Then why Benno the Mafia shylock? Because Benno was there when she decided to accept one. If the trial run worked out, Amo hoped to do better. Fewer bookings this year, no big money jobs that hiked her income, not one TV commercial that paid residuals. How did *they* know she was thirty?

She made up as she did for modeling jobs—skin smoothed, eyes curved, lips melted—because this was certainly a job of sorts. Once again she transmuted the lost Maruvian kid into a bright glittering Earth queen in a Pakistani negligee. She put on the black Jackie Kennedy wig requested (demanded) by Benno. She looked like a whore.

Amo held her pounding wrist and closed her eyes. She was having a severe case of nerves, aggravated by the jangling signals W.R. kept sending, which she ignored. Checked the clock. Due in ten minutes. She felt like a bad child about to be punished. Why did she call sleeping with an old friend—well, an old client—whoring around? Because she'd never have sex with him if he didn't pay her.

The buzzer rang. "Jackie?"

"Come on up." She rang him in with false gaiety, smoothed the wig, and glared at herself with fierce contempt. Amo had determined to beat the system of her Maruvian personality, to relinquish all tenderness and become as thick-skinned as the town.

In came Benno, a gray praying mantis with glasses on. No older than thirty-five, he looked as if he'd been unearthed by a Mediterranean dig in the midst of inscribing tiny figures on parchment in a dark tunnel by the light of nothing but his yellowed eyes. Then thrust onstage in a garish suit. Small wonder he liked voluptuousness.

"Hey, Jackie, ya look tough. Head by Jackie, body by Raquel—some combo." Benno circled her waist and Amo stiffened at the touch. "Ya oughta dye it, like I told ya. Ya'd make a mint." Benno clicked open his briefcase. "Here, I brought ya some vino and king crab. Ya like king crab? I'll fix it for ya later if you got mayonnaise and onions. Mind if I use the phone?" Benno loosened his tie and his Adam's apple worked compulsively.

Smiling, Amo swept her arm toward the phone. It helped to know he was nervous too.

"Hello, honey, is Mommy there?" Benno made kissing sounds. "There's your kiss. Get Mommy. . . . I love you too, Annie. Call Mommy now. . . . It's me, Nita. I'll be home at eight. . . . Working, whaddya think? For dinnah, yeh. Aw, knock it off, Anita." Benno hung up. "One more call?"

"Be my guest." Amo sipped wine and suddenly remembered the time Benno tried to rape her. He'd come to the D.O.D. to shoot pinups and nudes for his mail-order business, then refused to work. "You know why I'm here," he'd said, and grabbed her and wrestled her down to the bed. Amo kicked her way up, grabbed his camera and ran out on the landing naked and heaved the camera down the stairs. "You get out of here or I'll call your wife," she shouted back to the apartment. He came chasing out after his equipment and passed her, galumphing down the stairs, just as other tenants' doors inched open. Amo whipped back into her pad and locked the door.

Break their valuable machines—the car windshield, the camera. That's all she could do. An hour later he phoned apologetically. She met him at the bottom of the stairs and he paid her half fee and she didn't hear from him for a year. Finally she started posing for him again; he was older now, not so cocky, he said. Then he hit on the black Jackie wig. Now Amo was letting a man who had attacked her pay her to submit, and assuming a false identity to attract him.

"Yeh, Lisa," Benno was saying, "yeh, yeh. . . . Ya know I do, baby. . . . Man, ya're the all-time suspicious broad. . . . Ya disappoint me, Lisa. After all this time, how much trust ya got in ya boy, hey?" He winked at Amo. Baawwwk, went the receiver. He stuck his finger in his ear. "She hung up. That takes care of that."

Amo handed him his wine and they clinked glasses.

"Well, kiddo, here's to us, hey?" Benno leaned and they kissed awkwardly with bonehard mouths. "Gotta do better than that, Jackie."

His thin arms and skinny ribs imprisoned her like cold iron bars. Annoyed at her own reluctance, Amo threw her arms around his neck, closed her eyes so she wouldn't have to see him, and kissed him soundly, surprised that he didn't smell bad.

"Din't think I'd ever get you, kid." Benno smiled, sunken eyes glossy with greed. The pleasanter he tried to look, the more menacing he seemed. He put his dry scaly hand on her breast and her heart beat like a trip-hammer. "Ya really dig old Benno, hey Jackie?"

She swallowed. "I'll refill the glasses." She held her wrist that ached from W.R.'s continual signaling.

"We can't ball standing up." Benno took off his jacket and tie. Strapped under his arm was a shoulder holster with an automatic in it. Benno slung the belt on the floor.

"It's got a gun in it," Amo said, surprised.

"Aw, I thought it was a candy bar," Benno snickered.

She hated small black pistols. They were like slick oily snakes that could turn on her and spring. "Would you put it in the closet? I can't stand guns in the bedroom."

"Broads!" With swaggering disgust, Benno carried it to the closet and dropped it on the floor.

"Is it loaded?"

"What's the sense of toting an empty rod?"

"It might plug my fur hat." She mustered a chuckle.

"Safety's on."

"Do you have to carry it?"

"I'm in a rough racket, baby. Nobody pays to take a peek at my ass."

"We cheeky types have all the luck, don't we?"

"Whaddya mean?"

Amo forgot she couldn't talk to him. "Nothing—just a play on words."

"Don't play no words on me, hey?"

Amo sank onto the bed, lounging into a pose, chest out, tummy in. Suffering, denying she was suffering, forcing herself.

Without his jockey shorts, Benno was as narrow and dank as a tenement hallway that had never seen the sun. The hair on his body was scruffy and grew in irregular patches. He resembled an eel, boneless and flaccid, with a stick stuck in him for sex. She felt sorry for his body.

"Lisa says I come too fast"—his Adam's apple gulped away—"so I get her all ready to shoot before I put it in. I been wigged on ya for a long time, Jackie, so I know I'm gonna go right off."

"That's all right, Benno," smiled Amo, relieved to know it would be over so soon.

"So if ya want me to go down on ya—"

"I don't need it," she lied.

She lay back on the bed in the Jackie wig and he was over her, sucking on her lips, her ears, her breasts. Amo felt like a prisoner of war undergoing enemy torture and divulging no secrets. The jelly from her diaphragm faked lubrication. Finally he put it in and she thought, it won't be long now. Since she was a paid employee, she did her work. As he breathed faster, so did she, faking excitement. He came fast and she faked a half orgasm at the same time.

"Did ya come?" Benno panted.

"Halfway," she lied; she wasn't an intolerable liar.

"Ya beat that Lisa by a mile. I could get hung on ya, kiddo, if ya ain't a nag."

Amo laughed. You only nag a man you care about.

Benno fixed the king crab and they had more wine. Now that it was over, Amo felt pretty good. She'd passed her self-styled initiation into whoredom. She'd discovered she could sleep with anybody in the world: she'd just proved it. It was like having a built-in insurance policy you could always fall back on. If Benno didn't appeal to her, at least he wasn't besotted with perversions like Malachi.

They finished eating. "Where's the money?" Amo asked.

Benno looked distressed. "That ain't polite, Jackie. You find the loot on the dresser after I'm gone."

There it was, tucked under the ashtray. A few moments of horror for a hundred bucks; brave Amo. It was no more threatening than posing nude for a camera club of five Hard Hats who are getting angry because she stands and sits modestly. No more distasteful than knowing the big deal photographer expects her to sleep with him after a big money job, because he could've given it to someone else who would. She was a dirty girl in a dirty business, no doubt about it. If she was going to tease coldly, she might as well capitulate the same way. It seemed a natural extension of her modeling game.

"Thank you, Benno," she said kindly, nodding at the money.

"Ya dumb broad," Benno leered. "Where's ya manners? Like it's cheap!"

"Sorry." If she was a real Jackie and that was real sex

to Benno, she underestimated the male capacity for delusion.

He dressed and kissed her good-bye at the door. "I'll call ya next week, Jackie. Keep ya nose clean, hey."

Alone, Amo fondled her fast hundred. "Ha!" she snorted and wheeled about. She might as well get something for all the instant sex she was putting out. The only time she didn't feel like a whore was when she was being paid.

In the mirror she saw a phony she condemned without recognizing. She ripped off the matted wig and her face jumbled about and resettled into a different set of features with different color skin. A blonde with a serious, disillusioned face emerged, a face that looked as if it could not sustain another blow.

"Where *am* I?" she asked her image, dizzy with the changes, and fell on the bed in dismay. She felt as if she were suffocating, as if her arms and legs were being stuffed into her mouth and she was helplessly consuming herself. "What am I doing to myself? What?" She repeated the question sternly, hoping it might enlighten her.

"Oh, who cares?" she shouted. "Who cares?"

Nobody did. Not even W.R.   W.R. wouldn't answer.

Chapter 18
Nudies

Don't think before breakfast, Amo warned herself. Move! As soon as her feet hit the floor, she fell back on the bed wishing she never had to do anything at all but sleep. She'd curl up on a silver chafing dish with neon lights all around, and people would stop by and say, "Isn't it beautiful?" and she'd yawn and snore. "Thanks," she'd say and roll over. No more nudie movies, no more novel, just gorgeous everlasting Exhibit A.M.O. Once in awhile, if her wrist was tucked under her chin, she might break down and whisper to W.R.

Flat on her back on the mat, Amo legged-up, sat-up, twirled, bounced, and flexed. With the light off she thought she was safe. But across the street, with his light off, her neighbor flattened himself against the windowsill and rubbed. As he aimed his binoculars at the convolution in bra and panties, he rubbed till his loneliness was spent.

Suddenly Amo lost her fictional essence, her seething meaning, and became what she was—a tiny figure on the floor in a furnished room, along among the millions, almost always alone. She sank without a trace into her daily lonesome hell. In the hour before waking, she'd dreamed they were throwing shit in her face, she was sinking into quicksand of shit, up to her mouth. She woke up gagging and tried to cover herself with perfume.

They drove to the nudist camp for the second day of shooting on the Nudie. It was Amo's fourth Grade Z movie, and she had the lead. The producer was Old Left, the cameraman had been with the CIA in Laos, and his assistant with the Peace Corps in Nigeria. Vista Vue Nudist camp—cabins, pool, scrawny brush covering a hillside—offered every variety of handicap, physical and mental, including one chap without a penis.

The crew had to disrobe as well as the star. "For once, *I* get to see something!" Amo shouted with delight. She made a camera of her hands and shot them from every embarrassing angle, including choice close-ups, as they tried to cover up.

"Amo takes off her bra and—kerplunk," said Marty the producer.

"Marty takes off his pants and—ping," Amo made a tiny sound. They all fell about laughing.

They shot pool play, strolling and blueberry picking, shuffleboard, volleyball—Fun & Games. That was Amo's acting chore—to make it fun, ignore the hardening pricks, and act everybody's favorite secretary who becomes a nudist. Bouncy, bouncy.

"Amo, I can tell you love your work," said Marty. "You're so natural."

As Amo rested by the Vista Vue pool, a young paterfamilias stared at her and his stalk bloomed tremendously, wife and kiddies beside him. Amo turned away and stared up into legs and crotches walking by. She put on her bra so the sun wouldn't burn her breasts. A shock went through the place. Officials came running from everywhere.

"What are you doing wearing that bra?" asked the manager, tits hanging over her waist.

"Why not?"

"You're being very provocative," scolded a staff member, his belly so bloated you could stick a silver dollar in his navel.

"And we don't like it," said another.

"It's a medical problem," Amo announced seriously.

They conferred together, scowling, and finally went away.

Several guys came over and asked for her autograph. A minor luminary, halfway between a whore and a movie star.

Turning her head to her wrist, Amo whispered to W.R. "Make a movie of my life, W.R. I'm tired of all this shit."

W.R. rumbled a bit.

AMO: "Come on, W.R. Are you speaking to me?"

W.R.: "Hhrrumpff."

AMO (impatiently): "Well, if you want games—"

W.R.: "All right, A.M.O. What's on your mind, so called?"

AMO: "W.R., let's make a movie of my life—so I'll know I'm here."

W.R. (disgustedly): "Brilliant. You'll see our class film when you come back. Just ask for A.M.O. #309."

AMO: "But, W.R., I mean *now*. I want to be Liz and Dick, Warren and Julie, Eli and Anne, Yoko and John—"

W.R.: "So do they, I feel sure."

AMO: "But I'd rather be Liz & Dick wanting to be Liz & Dick. It's at least closer."

W.R.: "But you're in a movie *now*. I thought you hated this Nudie business."

AMO: "I do. I mean *my* movie, my own personal movie to watch, so I can see myself in action all the time. So I'll know I'm here. Like Jackie. She doesn't do anything. They record it. She knows she's here when she sees her face in the papers. Not like a model—like a celebrity . . . a phenomenon. Then I could watch the scene with Benno again. As a movie, it'd be great—the tension, the distaste, the fakery. Would it look phony? All the other scenes—all the men—I could watch and have with me. To run a reel for company. To have a friend."

W.R.: "Sad—sad, what you're coming to. We had such high hopes. . . ."

AMO: "But what's so awful—?"

W.R.: "You're going too far, A.M.O. You're becoming a sexual megalomaniac, like the rest of them."

AMO: "Didn't you advise me to develop my ego? The problem is No Identity. Unless they buy the novel . . . No Identity. I put it all in work—like you said—and forgot the love stuff. I'm lonesome, W.R."

W.R.: "And now they don't accept the work. (Sigh.) It's only a matter of time, A.M.O. They don't know what they're seeing when it's unknown—unimagined by others. But there must be some Earthman who has a glimmer . . . of the unknown, who's conceived the possibility—"

AMO: "I don't care. I'm going to fall in love."

W.R.: "With whom, if I may be so bold?"

AMO:"Well . . . I received from Timmie in Lon-. don more or less the same letter I wrote Eloy in Salamanca, which reminds me I no longer have to write Nacho in Mexico. I'll transfer it, according to who's available."

W.R.: "Who is available?"

In her bag with the morning mail was the latest card from Sandy in L.A.—an abstract of a broken heart, bearing the legend, THE PAIN OF THIS AMO COOVE WITHDRAWAL. He'd visited over Christmas.

AMO: "I'll write Sandy, W.R. Did I tell you he proposed—marriage?"

W.R. (sounding bored): "Ummm."

AMO: "What a jolt— to be proposed to when you're not paying attention, though I liked him in bed."

W.R.: "You were very rude. 'You don't even know me,' you said, like an accusation."

AMO: "The problem was Nacho, W.R."

Nacho, whom she'd met two days before Sandy in Mexico, Nacho whose Aztec profile and vulnerable

body were regularly passed by the black brute fur of
bulls with horns that hooked in tricky ways. *"Pero,
digo,* Amo, I love you in *Inglés* but not in H'Spanish,"
he said when he came to Nueva Yorrrk in February.
"You never hear me say *te amo*—be honest—do you?
You no find one Mexican man that marry you—you
don' have ze language, ze custooms. You don' have
custoom to be always in ze home. What you know of ze
home? Nahsing. You live independent—like ze man."

The pain of this Nacho Azcarraga withdrawal. So
she lost Nacho and by the time she wrote Sandy in
L.A., he was married to his Swedish maid.

The Nudie company had to stay over to shoot the
next day. Amo's cabin turned out to be . . . that of
Marty the producer. She slept in the bed with him and
fought him all night. They both looked mottled the
next day. This film was also very big around Times
Square, where for three months Amo titillated the
lonely souls who live in furnished rooms on the West
Side and come to the flicks to sit eight feet apart and
masturbate.

Chapter 19
The Co-op

At home in the D.O.D., Amo reread the letter from Timmie with its aristocratic scrawl and banal sentiments, Timmie, whom she'd met on the beach at Torremolinos strumming his guitar, singing *"Yo Vendo Unos Ojos Negros,"* and visited at the family manor in Kent. But in the meantime she'd fallen for Eloy the surgeon from Salamanca, who'd slithered down next to her on the black sand. Eloy, whose face was straight out of the Prado. Beside him as he sang *lento, profundo* *"Pena Penita Pena,"* walking past night gardens, holding a jasmine to her nose, then his, and far below the globes of fishing boats like stars in the old Mediterranean. At the outdoor *lugares de noche* where they danced, he always had a hard-on. Everyone did; it was complimentary local custom.

Eloy halfway asked Amo to marry him, by letter where it was safe. Timmie, though, he'd marry the girl who lived in the palace across the street. She'd visit Eloy this summer, if he was free. But she knew he wanted to marry one of his own just as Timmie did. Yes, she was a lark, a freak, everybody's Number Two girl friend. She'd never loved *any*one like she did Eloy, now that she was focused on him. What she loved most in Earthmen, he had—nimbleness, vibrancy, soul. As did Nacho . . . and Sandy . . . and—she was in love with all of them, truly, and could do about any of them individually.

Far easier to fall for Earthmen across the water, below the border. Here in alienated NY, NY, who was there? Benno. Duane the hippie stockbroker. Since he was so horny and so married, maybe he should help her out too. Amo was too exhausted from modeling in the day to write at night. She wanted to simplify her life.

So why not get three or four of them to keep her— at $100 a month apiece and see them each once a week. No—three times a month. That way she'd be supported, she'd see three different men a week, and the tab wasn't enough to hurt anybody. She could write in the daytime. All day. What luxury!

Russ the Wall Street lawyer phoned to make an appointment. She almost slipped up and asked him tc join her Co-op, but why mess up a good thing? Russ was a steady client. He shot Polaroids of her about twice a month at $40 for the hour.

Duane called. He and Amo had gone together before his marriage, till they had a fight—about the girl he married—and she yanked the St. Anthony's medal off his neck and he tried to throw her out the window, but it was closed. Duane looked as much as possible like a Hell's Angel, and drove his Caddy like a bike that leaped.

"Listen, Duane, $100 a month is nothing to you," she said when he resisted.

"But we're buying a co-op for seventy-five and the maintenance runs seven hundred a month."

"You're so fucking rich and I'm so miserable poor . . . that I just can't afford to see you," said Amo, "if you won't help out. The only thing I have is Time—and why should I waste it on a married man?"

"That's out front. I dig that, baby," he crunched in his fake hood's voice. "I suppose I can swing it for awhile. How's Tuesday?"

"—okay." She hesitated.

"I've got some great hash. *Ciao*, baby."

Of course now she had to sleep with him.

A famous writer, Bart Geller, called and she told him about her Co-op and he came by. He couldn't join, he said. He was really very well married and single girls were honored by his mere presence in their humble arms. But he offered her $50 to go down on him and she accepted, which was dirty of both of them. She accepted because she didn't want to sleep with him which was why he offered—because he sensed he didn't turn her on and resented it. He tried to come in her mouth but she gagged and pulled away.

"Ugh! It tastes like glue," said Amo.

"You'll never be a good cocksucker till you learn to lap it up and swallow it." His eyes narrowed, putting her on.

"Don't think I'll try." Geller left and Amo felt soiled. No to the Nudie producer; yes to Geller. Well, she liked his book.

Jay called, the TV correspondent she went out with last week for the first time. Jay had qualities Amo liked except he was an American, which he couldn't exactly help. Excited, she told Jay about her plan and invited him to be a charter member of the co-op.

"Are you serious, Amo?" He sounded disappointed.

"Yeaahhh," she said, all zapped up with desperate new alternatives.

After a moment he said sardonically, "It may sound corny to you, but I want love. If you really liked me, you wouldn't have to worry . . ."

"But I want cash on the line, babe."

"Steady money, you mean?"

"Yeeaahhh."

"Sorry, Amo," Jay said in a drowned voice, "I can't spring for that."

"Shit," she said. "I really like you."

He chuckled, "Well, then. . . ."

"I'm tired of slaving—night and day, day and night!" she shouted and slammed down the receiver. She blew that one too, all unawares. But she *was* tired. If she wasn't sleeping, she was writing, modeling, on Go-Sees, housekeeping, or screwing on a timetable. She never rested, never had free time. Between anxiety and overwork, Amo was very close to the edge. Maybe being thirty scared her more than she knew.

Models were old at thirty, writers young at thirty-eight. In the meantime, she had to eat. Amo remembered how she'd longed to be eighteen and twenty-one, then one day she was twenty-five and she felt ancient. Men don't like women, they like girls;

Amo knew that. She swore she'd be a girl forever. Somehow thirty seemed ten years older than twenty-nine, just as it did when shopping for $2.98 bargains. She had to convince herself she was younger today than she'd ever be again, that she was now Mature, that it was their problem (the boys), not hers. Anyway she'd lie about it.

Benno and Duane—at least $200 a month, minimum. She needed two more for real security. Marc called and Kemper, both kooks and both willing. She'd have to think them over carefully. The thing about keepers—that way you had steady boy friends who'd come back, since they were paying. If it was expensive, it must be worth something.

Like any local sex goddess, Amo had had too many men, too many voracious and fickle fans. She was weary of sacking the town, suckling half the city. Then Helmut called, a Latvian painter she'd known on Ibiza who reminded her of Timmie the Englishman. He'd jumped ship in Puerto Rico and was down the block in a phone booth on Broadway.

Helmut came by with his long orange mane flying and they went down to the Village barefoot and rolled around a couple of bars, rapped with the folks, sang *"Mustafa, ya Mu-u-sta-a-fa"* dancing down Waverly, roared home high on people and made love. Helmut went back to Berlin and bought a bar. He neglected to tell Amo he'd slept with a whore in P.R. because although it was dripping, he didn't get the results (clap) from Public Health till he left her place the next noon. Amo got the clap.

Not that she knew it. Nor did the doctor at dawn five

mornings later at Roosevelt Emergency, who called it cystitis. Amo, who hadn't slept all night from the tingling virulence that she could feel growing, suggested clap, but he poohpoohed it. Her own doctor said urethritis and sent her to a specialist who did $75 worth of urological tests rather than listen to Amo's symptoms. As the attack weakened her system, the urinary pain was intense (her diaphragm covered the inside, so she got it where a man does).

Finally Amo heard about Public Health, a dreary decent place where there were many fags and only one other girl awaiting treatment. She and the girl were as embarrassed as the fags were blasé. They shot her with penicillin *then* took tests, told her to hold off on the sex and drinking, said the private doctors were a menace about VD. Amo spent a pure month hating sex and many doctors. She refused to pay the specialist's bill. She wrote him she'd like to smash his head with an X-ray machine and send it down to pathology for urinalysis.

Phone rang. It was Amo's agent, who called to tell her the novel had been rejected again. Twice, in fact.

Tears filmed her eyes. Why did nobody want her special knowledge? That's what she was here for, here to propagate. Maybe W.R. was wrong and she simply had no talent. Amo paced about the D.O.D., her one-room jail, and looked outside for something worth her eyesight. She felt like crumpling over the windowsill—just lean till more of her was out than in, and gravity would do the rest.

Outside, the same bad abstract—red and brown

rectangles with windows with people behind them desperately looking for *something*, while trying to hide from the prying eyes of their neighbors. With wild stunted gaze, yearning for breezes ruffling trees, for grass smell and birdsong. For green. Green shot through with sunlight.

Frustrated by acrid gray, they watch their ineluctable neighbors and hope they'll at least do something obscene. Amo thought about flying in the window and fucking them, or from where she was, a dart in the heart would finish off that man staring at her, and the other one too (up two windows and over four), perhaps send them reeling out the broken panes to the sidewalk, dead and squooshy as garbage. At her command, couples fell out the window, locked together—splat on the sidewalk. Amo picked at random, emptying out the building—splat, splat. She even had several men swan-dive from the roof. The imagined dead were all men, except for the couples and the lone girl who'd fall and splat again and again, that she recognized as herself.

Across the street the Chinese man was masturbating again, a naked yellow Buddha aiming at her from his tiny room with the bare bulb emblazoning his act. Amo sighed and closed the curtain. Every time she looked out the window at dusk, he was there. Why did nobody want her work? Or her love? Only her body.

Amo turned off the lights and leaned against the full-length mirror—her breasts pressed against other dark breasts, her arms raised to other arms, her face against the cold glass, crying.

Unwanted in her essence, her fictional meaning. Amo, the Chinaman, and most of the window people. She had to stay out of the kitchen because of the knives, the kitchen knives she imagined jumping into her. She didn't know whether she'd kill herself or somebody else. All the same. No . . . no, of course it wasn't. But if she killed herself, she'd damn sure take somebody with her—somebody good, somebody big, that Earth watched and listened to, like it didn't to Amo.

On the mantel was the *banderilla* from the *corrida* when Nacho dedicated the bull to her. The festooned tip was covered with dried blood. She picked it up and tested the point on her arm, ran it down to her wrist, and W.R. screamed.

Chapter 20
Suffering in the Subway

"You've got to stop running and let somebody love you," Whitney said and pressed Amo's head to his chest.

Amo popped back up. "I feel more comfortable looking at your eyes."

"No, you don't. Relax."

Face crushed against his Cardin suit, for a fitful moment she stayed. "But I forget whose chest it is." What was he up to, eyes falling into her swooning with love—one of those German Greek God Vikings you never expect to see in real life.

How could a man so striking be a psychoanalyst? How could he not? The old gods claim their own. Whitney had a private practice in his own East Seventies town house; he was divorced and had a son. Perfect, too perfect.

Whitney hugged her, laughing. Blonder than she, his blue-sky eyes shimmered with change—enlightenment, puzzlement, affection, and zeal. Missionary zeal to conquer the far shores of personality. Like a clear blue day at the beach, nothing ominous about him.

Not like Malachi's black Irish-Jewish diamonds of eyes masking devious undulations inside the head.

"Freudian?" Amo asked.

"Existentialist," he replied.

Except Dr. Whitney Webb seemed too pure and zealous, too unfettered, too casually aware of his noble bearing.

Phone rang. "Who? . . . Oh, yes, Wacky Jackie. . . . How's Benno, my Mafia man? Okay, I won't say Mafia if you'll drop the Jackie." She turned away from Webb's inquisitive gaze. "Yeah, Friday's okay. Don't forget the— . . . Ah ha ha," she laughed, "don't be so touchy."

"Why are you doing that to yourself?" Whitney asked, eyes level, unshocked.

Amo pealed with laughter. "I need the scratch. It's my Co-op Plan. Want to join?" Too tan, too blond, too tall and fit; he'd never go for anything so sleazy.

He took her hands and kissed her gently on top of the head. "I think you should stop trying to hurt yourself."

Phone rang again, and he laid his eyes on her and tightened his grip on her hands, but she pulled away, frowning.

"This Amo Coove, the famous nude?" a roughie enquired.

Very formal, "This is she."

"Ya know what I'm gonna do fer ya, baby doll"—he snarled in pure rage—"I'm gonna slit ya throat fer ya. Slit it from ear to ear—"

Amo dropped the phone, clutching her throat. She

told Whitney, who yelled into the receiver, "We're having you traced, buddy," and the man hung up.

Shivering, she leaned against Whitney, looked out the window above the café curtain and saw several men on the roof across the way. Them . . . or the Chinaman . . . or the creep, Bernie, most likely . . . Malachi come back . . . or even Benno, or the movie producers, or— Too many possibilities. Choked with possibilities.

"Does that sort of stuff go on all the time?" asked 6'2" blond blue.

"No, usually they want to eat me up or fuck me to death," Amo trembled.

Whitney picked her up and carried her to the bed. "Let's lie down and rest a bit." He stroked her blonde hair and her forehead, her neck and shoulders till she smiled with slight peace. He seemed to think she was a WASP like himself, straddling the ethnic bedrock of the city, above it, yet an outsider. He'd tried to integrate in his marriage, a move based on pity and superiority. How naïve of him to expect Chelo to be grateful.

"Let's take off our clothes," he said.

"Why?" Odd that taking off her clothes before a strange man still appalled her, yet she always felt better naked.

"It seems the natural thing to do." Even on her back, her tits stuck up. He wanted to see.

"Yes, doesn't it?" Amo agreed, ripping off garments and tossing them over the side. Webb's clothes ended up neatly in order on the desk chair, as if it were a clothes tree.

Some body. Just the kind Amo liked—tan muscular chest and shoulders, long legs, white bikini left from last summer with what looked to be a fairly impressive centerpiece. She inhaled him, her eyes absorbed him, trying not to stare. White-blond hair on the arms and calves, none on chest and thighs. She felt suddenly incestuous and uncanny; he could be her Maruvian brother. Or W.R. embodied on Earth. Now, why did she say that? She'd never seen W.R.

"I've never made love with an analyst," was what she said.

He got hard just looking at those breast mounds with the Eye of God staring at him, commanding him. "We won't make love," Whit said. "I'll just put it in you for a little while."

Which he did, so she must have been ready.

Amo was pleased he was substantial enough so she wouldn't have to condescend to like him. Then she remembered it was the fertile time of the month, and she with no diaphragm. "Shoot, I haven't slipped up like that since I was pregnant five years ago."

"Aren't you on the Pill?"

"No, they took me off it for good when I had cancer."

"You haven't missed much." His eyes welled with sympathy. "Relax—I can control myself. You have to learn to let up on yourself a bit."

"Maybe so." She luxuriated in helplessness and

trust—neither of which had ever worked out for her—for perhaps five full minutes. His behind was smooth and silky. Unfortunately he did what he said. He stayed on his elbows and pumped it in and out leisurely without touching her otherwise, his heroic body hovering over her, she marveling at his dorsal latiserae. About the time she started getting really involved, so did he and he had to pull out to keep from coming in her, so she didn't come.

As she was douching, he walked into the bathroom. "Get out of here," she laughed.

"I want to help," said Whit. "It's friendly."

Amo blushed. "There's nothing for you to do."

He put the hole in the rubber bag over his finger. "I'll be the hook."

Whit held the bag aloft and the warm vinegary water descended from the bag to the long rubber tube to the douche nozzle which Amo inserted in herself. "What the hell, I'll show you a trick." Amo clenched her muscles and held the water inside for an amazing time, then spewed it all out at once.

They both cackled.

"Do it again," said Whit.

She did. They hooted and giggled like kids. "How about in syncopation?" Amo suggested then said quietly, "You're the only man who's ever watched me douche."

"I don't think you get to know people very well," Webb said.

She made a gray face in the mirror.

"You'll never know how lovely you really are," he

said sadly. "When you look in the mirror, your face
goes grim. Here—look at me, then right to the mirror,
without changing expression."

Playfully Amo tried it but as soon as she turned from
him to her image, her face lost its play. She could still
do it for the camera eye, but not for herself.

"That's what you think of yourself," Webb explained.

"I know."

"Why?"

"Because they haven't bought my novel."

He snickered in dismissal. "That's not why. It's
because,"—he put both hands on her shoulders—"you
haven't fulfilled yourself as a woman."

"Bullshit," said Amo, shaking off his grasp. She
collapsed, with a leap, onto the bed, Whit beside her.

Phone rang and she grabbed it. "Hello," she
hollered.

"We're willing to up that to $500 a day for three
days," said the nacreous soft voice.

"But why?" said Amo. "I understand everybody
gets $100."

"You're well known."

"I know this is corny," Amo said, "but I don't want
to be in a porno movie, at any price—"

"You may not think it," the man simpered, "but it'll
help your career . . . turn people on." Amo sighed
wearily. "I've told you for the past week the answer is
No. No. If you phone once more, I'll call the precinct."

No response.

"I got our conversations on tape," she lied.

"My, my, my," the movie man said softly and hung up.

Stroking her, Whitney said, "You have such a beautiful tender body. I'm sorry you have to lead such a hard life."

With that, Amo started sobbing. "Sometimes I feel like slumping over the windowsill. Fall out—bash, it's over."

"But why?" He seemed genuinely concerned. "I read a story of yours a few years back. You have ability."

"That and a token," said Amo. "Suffering in the subway, that's my lot. The other day I stood in the front car with a tiny Puerto Rican child watching the train nose through the dark tunnel—little waxen lights here and there. You could pop them out by spitting a little way and the train would wander underground lost forever. I sat down suffering and realized suddenly that I was *always* suffering, aching, in pain. Ever since I finished the novel that nobody wants. And before too—for years and years." Amo had never talked this way with an Earthman. "I don't care if I live or die. I'd just as soon chuck it in." She felt so inept, unwanted, as if a giant foot pushed on her head.

"Maybe you were missing me and didn't know it," Whitney said softly.

"Or worse—did." She squeezed him hard, then pulled away so as not to offend by overdoing.

"You don't have to go away." Whit pulled her back and cupped her head to his chest.

Amo almost rested.

Chapter 21
Whitney Saves

They couldn't go to the town house because it turned out Whitney was legally separated, not divorced, and his wife ("the bitch") already had one adultery charge against him, involving Beverly ("a real paranoid"), whom he'd just moved out a couple of weeks ago. But he thought the D.O.D. was artistic.

"Here's some new pictures of Adam." Whit handed Amo color shots of a blond child, quite tan, with huge black eyes.

"The sacred son," said Amo. "What a beautiful boy."

Whitney's eyes almost misted. "I'd do anything in the world for my son."

"Except stay with his mother," Amo cracked. "Who's this—the maid?" A small dark woman held Adam's hand.

"No, that's his mother." Whit flushed. "She's Latin—Puerto Rican."

"I'm sorry. She just doesn't look—"

"My type? When I met her, she was Rocky's mistress. Now she's a nut, a fanatic. She doesn't care about Adam—she punishes him all the time. Chelo *uses* Adam to try to hurt me. She won't let me see him on visiting day. Chelo's trying to destroy me. She wrote a dossier to the Institute full of bullshit about my sex life."

Amo blinked. "But, why?"

"Because of Jilly, the girl. Who's adopted, but not legally." He chuckled and took Amo's hands. "It's simple. You see, Chelo wanted to have another child after Adam, and it never happened. I'd determined I'd stay in the house till Adam was at least six, so he'd be in school and out of her clutches part of the time. Then Chelo heard about Jilly. That is, this cop's sister was pregnant with Jilly, and Chelo wanted to take the baby. I agreed, on one condition—that I be able to leave without recriminations, legal or otherwise."

"You agreed to what?"

"I signed the adoption papers to give the child a home,"—his eyes melted—"and left. I waited two weeks and walked out on the bitch—didn't even pack. Moved into the office till I got a tenant out."

Amo blinked a good deal more. "But you don't trade a child for a father—?"

"Why not?" he said brightly. "Only now they won't let Chelo go through with the adoption because I'm not in the house. So the kid has no status. It's just there."

"But what do you *feel* about her?"

"Nothing. I hardly know her."

Troubled, Amo walked away and silently inspected Baby, the palm tree. She jiggled the fronds because she figured Baby missed the breeze and liked being ruffled now and then. "Don't you, Baby?" She embraced the circle of fronds.

"You know why I really did it?" said Webb. "To get her claws off Adam—divert her attention."

"You mean you sacrificed the little girl on the altar of the sacred son?"

"For Christ sake, I gave the kid a home when it could've been aborted. Don't be so hard on me." He smiled, patting his lap. "Come here."

Amo wandered about the room then scribbled something on a piece of paper. She handed it to him when she finally sat on his legs. "Poem."

He read:

> Plants for babies,
> Words for flesh. . . .
> I've sold my whole
> Life—for a shriek,
> A scream of pain.

He nestled his head in her bosom. "Poor love," he said.

She hugged him to her and they fell in slow motion over on the bed.

After awhile Whitney said, "This time, let's do it my way. Be as relaxed as possible and don't squeeze."

"But I thought that felt good to men," said Amo, surprised.

Being an MD, he demonstrated with his hands. He curled one hand into a fist with a hole and stuck the index finger of the other into it. "When you squeeze—see—the penis can't get all the way in, and you're really just masturbating off the rim. Masturbating yourself and jerking me off, instead of letting me get deep inside."

"You felt like you were all the way in," said Amo who, presumably, might know.

"Not really," said Webb. "You have to accept me." He began kissing her and Amo thrust her eager pointed tongue into his mouth. "No," he said, "wait—don't rush things. Let me do that."

Amo's rejected tongue removed itself, and his stuffed into her mouth instead, which was fine with Amo. Then he kissed her breasts gently, bitingly, then sucked them hard. She didn't much like the look on his face. Very hard, too hard, taking not just the nipple but half the breast, and gnawing as if he were eating chicken at a picnic.

When she couldn't stand it any longer, Amo said, "Please! You're hurting me."

"No, I'm not," he assured her. "You have to give yourself to me. Just relax."

So she did. She relaxed and gave him her breasts and he kneaded them to dough, mauled them so they ached for two weeks. She'd gone limp like a drunk, and that saved her. When he put it in, Amo changed her passage from a vise into a cave, an empty deep waiting cave. Instinctively, she started to move with the rhythm.

"No," he said, "don't move. *I'll* do it."

"But it's hard not to move at all. It's natural—it makes it touch everything."

Webb lifted his weight from his elbows to his wrists, pulling out slightly. "My way, remember?"

"You want a sleepwalker, okay." Amo lay prone, without moving a muscle, and the less she did, the harder he got, this light hovering devil, in his eyes that asinine look of mastery she'd seen on so many men that always made her close her eyes to keep her mouth from twisting with irony. She knew the look they wanted in return—sort of limp ecstasy, eyes closed, so they could be the looker, the observer. Did he think he could pump hard enough to hurt her? The harder, the better she liked it. His chest and shoulders smelled of the sun—she breathed it in like a vacation—and she watched his muscles ripple slightly, almost effortlessly, as he thrust. His skin felt incandescent, fiery. As she got hotter, her body rose to meet and take his.

"No, don't," he said, "you'll ruin it."

Frustrated, Amo began to ache inside. With each thrust, pain—like blue balls—from not being allowed to respond.

"Now I'm all the way in," Whit whispered, thrilled. "Can't you feel the difference?"

So that's what it was; he was *in* farther, thought Amo. That's what caused the pain. He was trying to teach her something she didn't know—the pain of true penetration. It seemed to matter so much to him, and Amo wanted so much to matter to someone. To be allowed to love. Sacrificial, she felt—masochistic. Was that what it was to feel like an Earthwoman? He got much harder because she had submitted, and Amo felt very noble and powerful because she'd done that to him, for him . . . but then . . . then he came.

Hard breathing, sighing, snuggling, then when he recovered speech, Whitney said, "Did you have an orgasm?"

Amo wasn't sure. "Umm—*yes!* But it was so different."

"Like how?"

Improvising like mad, Amo said, "So much more —intense." Paused and added, "Not driving—bodily— but deep in the tissues." Was it true, she wondered? Did she mean it? Wouldn't it be wonderful if she did.

"You liked it—different?" His blue blue eyes were on her, the missionary converting the savage, waiting to fall into her with love if he heard the right answer.

"Yes." Amo decided she did—would.

Chapter 22
Asked Her to Marry Him

Whitney phoned. "The novel is great, darling. I couldn't put it down—read for five-minute snatches between patients. I love you for it."

"Really? You do?" Amo was overwhelmed.

"The New York parts I could smell and taste. But this Maruvian stuff—I don't believe a word of it."

"It's . . . fiction, Whit."

"But unbridled fantasy like that, it's a sign of detachment," he said with authority. "Schizoid detachment."

"From Earth?"

"From reality, my dear."

"Yes, I suppose so," Amo replied mildly.

"You mean it's *intentional*—to show her state of mind?"

Amo let out her breath. "Yes. Exactly."

"You *are* a clever bitch," he said caustically then laughed. "Let me know when you get my letter."

AMO: "Listen to this, W.R., and tell me your opinion."

W.R.: "Why does he *write*—from the East Side of town?"

AMO: "Whitney has always wanted to be a writer, a novelist. It's his dream, he says."

W.R.: "An old-fashioned boy!"

AMO (conspiratorily): "They all think they want to be writers."

W.R.: "No doubt because it's so easy."

AMO: "No doubt. Okay? It's long.

'The first time in my life that I have been truly a man. You did it, Amo. I think it was that you truly wanted a man and you didn't fight it. My fucking penis plunged and searched and coaxed and lurked till it found that spark and drove it on and on. It fought and raged and would not be denied. I drove some on further than they wanted to go or could stand to go believing that they wanted it, discovered that they couldn't stand it after awhile and I was killing them. Then it had to end. What madness—bleeding, unwanted passion. Amo, you are the very first and the only and the only only woman I have ever met who truly wanted to be a woman. Never has anyone of herself been warm. Never have I seen the look of deep, beautiful, warm love I saw on your face. Every other woman has either wanted to cling or control—control me like my bitch of a mother or spit me out then crawl inside of me. . . .

What do you think?"

W.R.: "He's no writer."

AMO (chuckling): "Still a toddler there. But what else?"

W.R.: "He's dangerous."

AMO: "Shoot! Every man I like is dangerous to *you*, W.R. Are you too jealous to be objective?"

W.R.: "He's pompous. Or does he have the planet's first ageless penis?"

AMO: "No—the same wavering stalk. He's just an Earthman—puffed with harmless ideas."

W.R.: "Harmless till he puts them into practice. Sounds like a very tricky Gobbler to me."

AMO: "Oh, W.R.! What else do I have?"

W.R.: "What does he mean by—driving women too far? By you being the first—everything? Is he sixteen?"

AMO: "Thirty-four. It's an Earth custom. Every time you fall in love, you claim it never happened before, or not so profoundly, and that all those who came before were unsatisfactory."

W.R.: "Inundated with fantasy, that planet."

AMO: "Totally. But wait—here's the important part.

> Come and live with me and love me
> forever. Not for just a little while, but always.
> I don't care how long or short forever is, as
> long as it is forever. You know there is no one
> more right for me than you. If that isn't true
> and made to last then what is the point to life,
> or me. Marry me, my love.

W.R.: "He doesn't seem to think clearly. Isn't he married?"

AMO: "He's being metaphoric—romantic they call it here. He wants me to live with him and marry him when his divorce comes through."

W.R. (static, with suspicion).

AMO: "He calls me his Dream Girl."

W.R.: "His what?"

AMO: "His queen, his cloud goddess."

W.R.: "Maruvian, do you mean? But you confirmed they don't know about us."

AMO: "No, no. It's fantasy again."

W.R.: "How can you fantasize a living being?"

AMO (enthusiastically): "Like modeling—like the movies. He says he forgot about his Dream Girl but that's what I seem to be, resurrected."

W.R.: "Then he doesn't know you."

AMO: "You're a cube, W.R."

W.R. (sternly): "Have you forgotten your mission?"

AMO: "Mission—pission. I'm no Maruvian. I want some Earthly satisfaction."

W.R.: "You're seeking security and protection . . . like a mere Earthling."

AMO: "Riiiight!"

W.R. (emotionally): "I can't tell you how disappointed I—we— no *I* personally am."

AMO: "But, W.R., I *did* it. I tried! And no one bought it."

W.R.: "And now he wants to . . . buy you and work on you."

AMO (furious): "You're so crude." She cut W.R. off with a slam that hurt her wrist.

Amo worked two trade shows back to back. One week she pitched TV Studio Vans for a Japanese firm at the Electronics Show. The next week she wore a low-cut potato sack to sell potato guns and ant farms at the Toy Show. Then she didn't have another job—not even a one-hour booking—for eleven days. As Amo got better as a model, unfortunately she got older as well. Her face was all too familiar; she was beginning to be overexposed. New faces, they wanted, and younger. Always younger. She asked W.R. if the Time Stopping Pill could be instigated on Earth, just once, for her. Ah ho, ah ho ha, W.R. laughed.

Amo paced about the D.O.D. You sit in your tattered loneness and take the passing horrors; that's what W.R. expected her to do. She looked out at the bleak sky, longing for the solace of blue. Always longing. What W.R. didn't understand was that she didn't care that much about herself alone anymore—propping herself up, being her own prod, to make a persona for . . . herself. Amo was ceasing to care, losing interest in herself and her mission. Going dry but for Whitney. No longer able to conceive of a We, then Whit happened along.

Outside, the tortuous river of metal clanked by, brakes squealing, farting fumes for those left behind as the traffic escaped the city, via the cruddy West Side.

Phone rang. Bill Thor, great American novelist back from Paris, discovered she lived three blocks away and wanted to come by instantly and celebrate. Bill Thor, my God—of course! There were so many things she wanted to talk to him about. Amo raced around fixing herself up, tossing stray jeans and sweat shirts into the closet.

All her adult life she'd been taken out to dinner and home to bed—what a great way to live! What a fantastic city! Where else could she pull off such a stunt? The turnover might be too fast but the supply was apparently endless. It took a city of eight million to supply Amo. An endless river of interesting men flowing past her door, and when she was thirsty, she drank. The D.O.D. was transformed into a cozy cave that surrounded her like a cantankerous mate demanding care, brawling and caressing at the same time, close as a cocoon. It was her riverbank where she rested when she was sated.

Could she leave her Dear Old Dump, her modeling business, her men, her role, her chic despair, her solitude, her independence, her old age and poverty and suicide, her keepers' Co-op for Whitney? A lone man. Of course not.

First-rate novelists do not tend to be tall, dark, and handsome but Bill Thor was—with broad shoulders, unsettling eyes, and black gobs of hair, all of which wavered at her as he entered cuddling booze and mix. Amo turned on like a laser ray of hope. She wanted to tell him about her novel, ask about the lit business. There were so many things only another writer understood. She wanted that intimacy and knowledge with somebody good.

They circled each other, mumbling pleasantries. Amo mixed the drinks and he sat down in the circle chair. As she handed him his drink, he reached for her leg but she scooted away and sat at the café table.

He fell forward out of the circle chair to his hands and knees and crawled toward her. Upon arrival, he tried to push her legs apart. "Come on, baby, let me eat you," Bill Thor said. "Then I'll leave. If you won't let me fuck you, at least let me eat you. You won't have to do a thing."

"Why don't you talk to me?" Amo kicked his hands away. "I'd like to get to know you."

"Come on, come on. Don't you know sex is communication?" Thor sat on his haunches, impatient. "Besides, I owe you that. I never did that to you."

"But we've both done that and everything else with other people, so what's so new about it?"

"But with *me*, baby—with me," said the oracle, reaching for her tits.

"But I don't *know* you." She elbowed him off.

"Sure you know me. You slept with me once."

"But that was a long time ago and you never came back, so I *didn't* get to know you."

"Ah ha, so it's all turned to vengeance, eh? Baby won't admit I hurt her feelings." Thor smiled with handsome superiority.

"Listen, I'm in favor of revenge and *of course* you hurt my feelings. But you're presumptuous to assume my interest is the same now." He sure knew how to turn a girl off.

"Oh ho, she *is* vengeful." Thor stood to refill his drink and tried to jam his hand down her blouse.

"Cut the shit, you clown!" Amo bellowed.

"Oooh hoo." He scooted away petulantly.

"Don't you ever talk to other writers about writing?" Amo asked, disappointed.

"Only the young and naïve do that. I don't rap about it, I do it."

"I wanted to tell you about my novel." Amo was still reaching for some soul in him. "There are so few people—"

"What for? Writers don't give each other anything. Writers are secretive, you know that."

"Small minds always think they have a hold on something unique," Amo said sadly.

"Talk to your agent. He's your crying towel."

"That's not what I meant."

As he passed her, Thor tried to tweak her mound by ramming his paw into her lap. Amo kicked at him with her leg and sent him flying off balance. He bounced himself off the wall with an ape grin, eager to scuffle.

"I've had enough." Amo leaped up and went to the door and opened it. "Get out of here."

"But, baby," Thor droned in seductive complaint, "what's better than sex?"

"Real sex, but that involves emotion." Amo stood her ground in the hall. "Get out!" she said loud enough for other tenants to hear.

"I'll take my bottles," Thor said churlishly and swept out past her.

"Oh, *do* take your bottles." So much for enlightening conversation with the great American writer.

When Whitney phoned, Amo said yes, with grati-
tude. Yes, love, yes.

Amo called W.R. to apologize. It took awhile before
W.R. would respond, as she'd known it would.

AMO: "Let me off, W.R. I want to be an average
woman. Let me be normal."

W.R.: "All right, A.M.O. We won't stop you."

There was a high-pitched silence.

W.R. (sadly): "Will you . . . keep calling in?"

AMO (subdued): "I don't know—if I should."

W.R. (pitch cracking): "You can, you know. I—I'll
miss you."

AMO (sobbing): "Me too. So long, W.R."

Stupid as it may seem, Amo cried and cried.

Chapter 23
Love

Mrs. Silverman phoned for the tenth time that day. Whitney motioned to Amo to pick up the extension.

"Since your home is your office, Dr. Webb, and we are forced to share our therapy with another person, I think you owe it to us to tell us who that woman is," Mrs. Silverman hinted.

"Ask me that on Tuesday in your proper time and I'll answer it," said Whit. Amo hugged him, laughing, and Whit scooted off to see a patient.

"Ready, Eric?" Whit called to a fag who followed him delicately up the gold-carpeted staircase. They went into the bedroom Whit used as an office and the door slammed.

Amo had sold the key to the D.O.D. for $300, bought a Mexican carved desk that looked like an altar, and moved into Webb's town house. East Seventy-sunny was a block-long haven of tree-shaded houses between the bank vault façade of Park Avenue and the jumble east of Lex. They looked like ordinary houses, which is what made them so rich and valuable on the crammed

East Side. Whit's was a four-story red brick with a round emblem like a seal of approval stamped above the entrance. No doctor's sign, of course.

The double living room alone was twice the size of Amo's apartment. It had two fireplaces and two chandeliers ("They need cleaning," said Whit) and served as the patients' waiting room. Upstairs were two bedrooms and baths. The back bedroom was Whit's office.

In her shorty nightie, Amo wandered downstairs yawning and bumped into an elegant middle-aged executive sagging wanly on one of the sofas. "Hi," she said, as his eyes widened, and spun down to the basement. The stone basement smelled like a cave with a pink kitchen in it. The back half became Amo's studio with her altar desk and round marble dining table and Baby, the palm, getting light from the French doors. The doors opened onto a cramped prison yard of a patio, walled on three sides by houses since it was on a corner.

Several panes near the doorknob were still missing from the time Beverly tried to break into the house. Whitney had spent the weekend with Amo in the D.O.D. When Beverly discovered he was gone, Whit explained, "She went into a rage-panic and climbed the fence and tried to break in, and cut her hand rather badly." She had been Whit's patient before her elevation to girl friend and, he said, "She hasn't been able to accept removing her dependency from me." Beverly was a Radcliffe Phi Bete who worked as secretary to a foundation head who expected her to service the corporate heads who serviced the foundation.

After her exercises and breakfast, Amo looked through the banisters to see a sexy mother and sullen daughter waiting above. She had to get upstairs to dress. She dashed up the stairs so fast they did a double take. All day long Amo dodged patients.

Whit disapproved of Amo's modeling and felt she should "devote her juice to her writing." So did Amo. She agreed to pay for her keep with housework. A one-man Co-op—what could be better? The three gold-carpeted floors of the town house had to be vacuumed around the patients, as well as the two spiral staircases. Also Amo had to vacuum the fourth floor, rented out to painter Gordon Brasil and his wife, because the maid had done that too. Whit fired the maid because, as he said to Amo, "What other responsibilities do you have?" Amo mentioned her writing but since the novel hadn't been bought, Whit wouldn't let that count.

Today Amo clocked the vacuuming at three and a half hours, using attachments for windowsills and molding in the living/waiting room. Since it was a doctor's office, Whit wanted it done twice a week. As she wiped her brow, Mrs. Chester-Coen came in doffing her mink jacket.

"I see you have a new maid, Doctor," said Mrs. Chester-Coen.

Amo leaned on the vacuum and glared at Whit standing behind his Spanish dining table desk. He was reading something. He smiled slightly but didn't look up. "Would you have any free time—?" began Mrs. C-C hopefully.

"I am the Doctor's girl friend," Amo gritted, "and I do this out of pure heart."

Then Whit flushed and gave her a mean eye. "Ready, Ruth?" he said to Mrs. Chester-Coen and trotted ahead of her up the stairs.

Amo heard a torrent of tears. "Oh, Whitney, is it true?" "There, there, Ruth," and the door slammed.

Out of pure heart tomorrow she had to clean all four johns. "Twice a week because it's a doctor's office," said Whit. "Here, let me show you." Whit had gotten on his hands and knees, scrubbed vigorously at a corner, got up smiling, pleased with himself, never to bend again. Amo tried it; he smiled down upon her and left. Then the furniture had to be lemon-oiled once a week, all that Spanish wood. "I didn't hire on as a galley slave," said Amo. "It's a doctor's office," the Doctor replied.

As Amo spiraled upstairs for her shower, she heard a plaintive moan from the office. "But I love you, you know that, Dr. Webb. How can you do this to me?" That would be Joan, the Vassar social worker. Doctor's voice: "But love doesn't have to be exclusive, Joan. You can love people in different ways." Joan, hysterically: "But she looks like a whore, a common tramp." Doctor: "She was a model, I told you." Joan: "Well, it's the same thing."

Sloat-bellied slut, thought Amo, reaching for the knob, ready to burst in.

They're *sick*, she warned herself, mentally ill. That's why they're here. All these hysterical paranoid ladies in love with the great Doctor; they seemed so much alike.

Amo fed Whit on the dot of seven since he liked to watch the Cronkite Show and had an eight o'clock patient. He ate the chops, sipped the wine, eyes on the tube. She knew not to speak till the news was over. At seven thirty she spoke to him, "How's Joan getting along?"

Silence.

Amo repeated the question.

"Too involved in social work, emotionally. I'm switching it to her boy friend," he said tonelessly, wan blond and tired.

"By way of you?"

"That's transference."

"Why not make her independent while you're at it?"

"I want her to be happy."

Amo scowled. "But you're an existential analyst, not a Freudian."

Whit shouted, "Let me rest—please!"

They sat till eight, Whit wiped out and glassy-eyed, Amo talk starved, swallowing every new idea that occurred to her. A congress of unemitted signals congested her throat. She wanted W.R. No, she wouldn't. Now it was Whitney and Amo, not Amo and W.R. At eight he shot up to see his last patient, an unfulfilled lady editor.

Amo did the dishes and he came back down at nine and flaked out behind the sports pages, staring at the good guys and the bad guys on TV. "Shhhh," he said when Amo tried to talk. So she read till she fell asleep in front of the set.

Whit woke Amo and they went up to bed. Once in bed, he reached for her breasts and she gave him the elbow. "Not when you don't speak to me all night."

An hour later there was a loud crash in the living/waiting room. They leaped awake. Whitney slipped on his pants and stumbled down the stairs, switching on the chandeliers.

"Beverly!"

She hadn't turned in her key. The vase was shattered.

Raging like a hyena in heat, Beverly headed for the stairs. "Let me at her! Let me go! I'm going to tear her eyes out."

Whit caught her around the waist and she clawed him, trying to scramble up the stairs.

Amo put on a minislip and bra and went out on the landing where she saw this small demon, thin and dark, rampaging toward her. Beverly wasn't very pretty.

"You left me for *that?*" screamed Beverly. "She's so . . . she's *nothing—!*"

Amo laughed.

"Your slip's on backward," said Beverly.

"It wouldn't be if you didn't come calling so late," said Amo.

"You're both wigged." Whit flipped Amo Beverly's key. "I'm going to walk Beverly home," he said paternally, holding her by both shoulders by way of restraint.

Beverly tried to snarl at Amo, and Amo tried to smile pleasantly, and Whit headed her out the door.

If Beverly had a key all along, why did she try to break in the back way? Amo knew why—she wanted to smash things, tear up the joint.

All the man-worshiping exploitable frightened ladies in love with the great Doctor. It set Amo to wondering if his practice were not based half on his looks, half on his authority, and on nothing else of any real significance. That night Amo dreamed Whit was having sex with someone else, which upset her, so she got him to stop to have sex with her, and he wanted to put his cock in her with the other woman's blood on it.

Chapter 24
Number One Whore

After six months together, of a Saturday Dr. Webb and Miss Coove strolled around Times Square to see Miss Coove in her starring opus, *Cathouse Rebel*. Forty-second Street jutted with marquees, like a giant line of Rockette tits offering treats. Below these nestled long dark caves where the treats were. Inside, the patrons were spaced sparsely for irrigation, about eight feet apart, no two together. The odor of semen permeated the place.

Amo blushed at what she had accomplished, blushed for Whitney. As they took their seats, the patrons leered anxiously at the well-dressed couple. There was Amo on the silver screen, bigger than life, looking bloated in the stomach, haggard of face. No one recognized her.

"You look like a whore," Whit said, shocked.

"I was *playing* a whore. I've always played a whore," said Amo. "It's my most popular role."

"You let people *use* you," he scowled. "You're trying to destroy yourself."

"The other girls look like whores too," said Amo.

"The head cameraman told me they used dirty film and dirty lighting for a sleazy tabloid effect."

"But why?" Whit was nonplussed.

"If they'd lit the set right and used quality film, everyone would have looked like an angel and not a whore." She watched herself shooting smack, being tortured by her pimp, and thought with great agony of the unwanted novel she'd walked through this hell to finish. To no avail.

"Looks authentic, all right," said Whitney.

So authentic that *Cathouse Rebel* became an underground classic and moved from Forty-second Street to instant revivals at the art houses.

At home the phone rang for Amo. It was best-selling writer Barry Josephson, back from Madrid, on his way to Mexico and he wanted her to go along. He was doing a bullfight book, part of which would be serialized in *Esquire*. "On whom?" said Amo.

"El Cordobés—he's fighting for six weeks in Mexico and South America, and we need a translator, among other things."

"He looks just like Bobby Kennedy!" piped Amo.

"Ought to be one of the great all-time blasts," said Barry. "Your Spanish still good?"

"Oh, sure." Amo's excited eyes gazed blindly at Whit.

"We'll be everywhere, with everybody. If you get bored screwing in Spanish, there's always plain ole Bare."

"Oh, Barry, I can't." She lowered her voice. "I've gone straight—I'm living with a shrink."

"So take a vacation." Blithe Barry. "At least, ask."

"Hold on." Amo skipped over to Whit who was stretched out on the waiting room sofa, staring up into a chandelier.

"These chandeliers really need cleaning," said Whit.

"Um, Whit, can I go to Mexico to . . . translate for the . . . bullfight season? With . . . this, um, friend, Barry, and El Cordobés?" Amo's hands twisted together like a kid who knows the answer is no.

"Do whatever you like," said Whit, reaching for the sports pages. "But don't come back here."

Her hands fell to her sides and her back slumped ever so slightly. "No, of course not, what am I thinking?" Amo sighed heavily and went back to the phone. "Barry, I can't do it. Whatever was I thinking?"

"Remember, I gave you first crack, Amo." Barry's voice was gruffer now, more businesslike, eager to get off the line and continue the pursuit.

"Yeah—"

"Hate to see you so boxed in, girl. Well—have a happy life."

"Sure, Bare." Amo added, *"Buena suerte—un beso por el matador,"* but he'd already hung up.

Whit slung down the sports pages, crossed his arms behind his head. "Can't you see they're trying to *use* you?"

"Man, I'd like to use El Cordobés awhile," Amo let out before she could catch it.

"You oppress yourself to the desires of others," he mused, "because you want their approval."

"Yes," said Amo, "apparently."

"You don't really want to sleep with that bullfighter, but you think the prestige would make everybody like you," Whit said soberly, blue eyes very large and vulnerable.

"It's over, baby. Let's forget it." Now she was truly sorry.

"What did you call me?"

"What?"

"You called me baby, didn't you?" Whitney laid the godhead eyes on her.

"I suppose so."

"I don't like it. I'm not a child."

"You sound like one," said Amo, then saw the red fury enter his face. "Darling angel cake honey pie sweetheart *corazón mi vida mi precioso bebe*—what's the difference?" She kissed him apologetically on the cheek, making loud smacking noises to placate and amuse him.

Up to bed they went, Whit twisting her waist from behind as Amo switched her hips elaborately with each step, singing, "*Que bonitos ojos tienes. . . .*" He goosed her and she collapsed on the stairs, giggling, squirming, rolling over. He fell on her and both of them slid down a few steps then scrambled up again, he trying to clutch her crotch like a bowling ball and hoist her up the stairs, Amo reaching through his legs and bouncing his balls, dribble dribble dribble.

Amo slung her clothes somewhere and leaped onto the bed, bouncing it like a trampoline. Whit jumped on top of her and clutched both her breasts in his hands like two giant foaming mugs of suds, and sucked and played and bit and gnawed, harder and harder. Finally Amo pushed at his shoulders and succeeded in lifting his head, his eyes like an animal caught at his meal by a larger beast.

"Why don't you go down on me," said Amo, "or at least touch me there with your hand?"

He touched her. "Because you're not excited there."

"But that's why—to make me excited."

"I've been kissing your breasts for five minutes, and you're still cold."

"It's because you've been hurting me, Whit. You're being too rough. Not much—but enough to cause pain."

"Nonsense," he said, incredulous. "Why would I do that?"

"You say you hate your mother," Amo said playfully. "Maybe you transfer it to me." She kissed his ear.

Whit roared with laughter and rolled around the bed. "If a patient said that to me! You don't know how much I let you get away with."

"I'm not your prisoner," said Amo coldly, starting to get up.

Whit caught her and pinned her shoulders. "You're my prisoner of love." He straddled her and returned to the breast play.

She reached down to feel his cock and he shifted slightly away. So she knew what he wanted—his way, with Amo the supine object who was also molten. She would have to get her entire stimulus from the tit play while he withheld the magic wand till he decided she

was ready. The measure of her love was that she could
do it—because he wanted it. She gave up the ghost,
gave him her body, translated every pain into pleasure,
psyched her response higher and higher.

Whitney watched her. Even when she was submissive, as now, Amo seemed to step outside herself like
some stealthy cat—immobile, paws together, waiting
with neither patience nor impatience for him to finish
his little game—his ravagement of this perfectly
willing, sensual, nubile, responsive creature—who
could turn it off and on, be here, there, or gone with
instantaneous, interchangeable effortlessness. She was
always there, ready to respond to a desire before he'd
even articulated it with his body. She was unbelievable. If he tried to hurt her, she gave in with
masochistic ooze and was never hurt. If he evaded,
feigned disinterest, she clamped on him and yanked it
out of him or coaxed it out with gentle sucking strokes.
She compensated for everything and he could not pin
her down. Like the GI's searching for the VC, he
thought. The white warrior unable to conquer the tiny
yellow whore. Do you love me? Yes, I love you veddy
mush, let me show you how mush, says she. How
could she? How can he believe her?

Being Maruvian, Amo was strong because she was
malleable. If he twisted her into a pretzel, when she
unwound, her muscles would be just a little stronger,
that's all. Or, put another way, she could come off
love. It didn't really matter what he did or didn't do.
She had learned to come off love, to her own surprise.

Off passion, not organs. That, more than anything, convinced her that her love was real.

That night Whit dreamed he and Amo were at an Institute party and he walked into the kitchen and Amo was sitting on the lap of that ham actor, Dr. Stefan Luks, and kissing him, her hand on his leg. Whit walked out of the kitchen and came home and threw all her things out into the street, only he couldn't figure out how to dispose of her altar desk.

Amo dreamed about a glass table with her few objects piled together in a sort of kidney on a small part of it, and waiting for Whit and Whit not coming, although people came and went. She shook awake and gripped him tightly. She cried out, he said, and quaked with a fear of loss and held onto him.

Whitney decided Amo's clothes were too scroungy, that she should dress up to her position as his esteemed mistress. He gave her $70 and told her to get a good dress at Bergdorf or Bendel's. Amo always felt inferior in fancy shops with well-dressed ladies. On the street she didn't feel such an outcast but here, in these artificially lit puffed cages of the establishment, she knew she was a failure—on their terms, of course, but also on her own. She had recoiled from getting it their way—respectable marriage to corporate man. But she had not succeeded in the novel, the alternate path she had hoped to show them. So she was a bum.

Amo tried on many chic, now, with-it dresses she hated but fortunately nothing fit. Besides, she needed everything—pants, tops, dresses, coat, and shoes. She went to the good shoe department at Bendel to get a pair of dress shoes Whit would like. Amo liked exotic ones with bright colors and weird shapes and wacky heels. She brought home a pair of purple-and-red suedes with a six-inch platform and ankle straps that made her feel like she was sailing through space again.

"Where do you think you're going in those?" Whit asked.

Amo returned them, agonized between five similar pairs of black kid pumps. She set them all out in front of her on the shoe department rug. She couldn't decide. She didn't know what he disliked; she didn't want to displease him with her gaucheness again. For an hour she sat and sweated in the good shoe department.

"How many times you got to try those same shoes?" the clerk asked angrily.

"Listen," Amo slipped a Times Square snapshot of Whitney out of her purse. "Which do you think he'd like?"

The clerk shrugged and walked off.

Finally the manager came over. "You spending the night, lady?"

Trembling with indecision, Amo bought the ones with the least shape and ornamentation. She guessed right. Whit thought they were subtle. Amo thought they were suburban, conventional, dull.

Chapter 25
Foxy

FAMOUS TIDBITS OF THE PAST, the cover of *Meat* magazine proclaimed in bold black letters. Amo opened it to the old nude of herself, considerably reduced in size, and wondered if it looked so dated to anyone else.

Miss Amo Coove, the Writing Tidbit—March, 196–, the legend read. A relic—the Stone Age Tidbit. The spaced-out N.G. writer, whore, bum. Unwanted. It might as well be her Post Office mug shot, head on, full figure: UNWANTED BY THE LIT BIZ, *Do Not Bring In Under Any Circumstances.* With the tapeworm of rejection eating her, Amo was beginning another novel.

A letter came from her agent, Curt Candidt, the blue letterhead the very shade of failure. It was a copy of a letter from Foxcroft Levy, Editor-in-Chief of mammoth Select House. It was long. It was an offer—a conditional offer. Amo shook so she could hardly read. It said:

May 20, 196–

DEAR CURT,

We here at Select are mightily impressed with *The Gobbling Deficiency* by your Miss Coove (is that right? Cove? Cave?) and think her device—the so-called Gobbling Deficiency—is a perfect vehicle for expressing the problems we all encounter with the factional hysteria of the age—from the Jewish mother to the American bitch to the Big Nurse syndrome and now, finally, the Lesbian hostility that is devouring us all in the name of Unisex.

Not to say anything so Freudian as Biology is Destiny (though evidence of male bonding would indicate), we came up with what we think is pretty much a coup of symbolic usage; that is, to be really effective—and rational in relation to the world today—the device should be switched from the Maruvian men to the Maruvian women, as an indication of the age-old female desire to overthrow man, the insidious power play of the spider that as we all know (from experience!?) kills its mate after lovemaking.

If she'd be willing to make that small—and realistic—adjustment, we are prepared to make her a firm offer of $5,000 on signing, $5,000 when MS is turned in, for a total of $10,000, which we feel is more than generous.

See you for lunch Thurs.

Best,

Foxy

Foxcroft Levy
Editor-in-Chief
Select House

(subsidiary of National Blowtorch)

Her agent wanted her to do it. Whit wanted her to do it. Foxy was all charm when she talked to him on the phone. Amo was thinking of W.R. and A.M.O.'s mission.

"It would be much more logical, baby," said Whit. "No one has yet disproved penis envy. In fact, feminine psychology is the apotheosis of penis envy."

"Who gives a damn about the little twingie? It's the man's relationship to the world that women want—for themselves, too."

"Exactly! But *men* are hunters, not women."

"I can't," said Amo, "because it *was* the men and not the women who suffered the Gobbling Deficiency, just as it is here. Men war and kill—women don't."

Paternally, Whitney felt her forehead for fever and went to take her pulse at the wrist. "I've been very patient, Amo, with this fantasy life you use in your writing, though I disapprove of it. Such expansive imagination is the first sign of a detached personality. Schizoid detachment. I've told you. I thought you understood that. But you seem to *believe* this Maruvian guff!"

Amo chortled. "If Freud isn't fantasy, neither am I."

Webb always ignored irrelevant remarks. "No one senses real fulfillment from fantasy adventure," he said kindly, taking her hands gingerly so as to avoid that strange wrist.

Amo knew W.R. was upset. She wanted very much to contact W.R., just to talk on an intelligible level again. Of course she knew W.R. would be opposed to the change. A real Gobbler technique, W.R would say. But she felt the decision should be her own, without W.R.'s moral support. W.R. wouldn't understand how desperately, how ferociously she wanted to be published after the long years of work. A published novelist—dream fulfilled, identity attained. From bum to professional in one tardy editorial stroke.

"Well?" said Whit. "If you change the Gobblers to women, I'll be much impressed with your rationality. Your logical sense."

"I can't change history, Whit." Amo felt her wrist quiet down.

"Eternal Eve,"—Whit glared thinly at her,—"with her bag of tricks."

"I'm going to turn down Foxy." Amo went to the phone and dialed her agent, moral fiber blossoming all through her.

"Wait now Amo." Whit pressed down the phone. "Don't rush into this."

Amo said stiffly, "*I* wrote the book, you hungry Gobbler."

That night Amo dreamt she was sentenced to jail for being a serious writer. It was a crime for a woman. "Why, why?" she kept pleading as the all-male jury smiled at her, winked, arms crossed. The Judge leaned down stately, "The egotism of serious creativity is forbidden to women." The mallet bonked like a blow and the male jury applauded as one. There she was behind bars, tiny and yellow, the VC whore.

Chapter 26
Househump & Dumptruck

After the phone call from his mother, Simone Webb, the renowned critic, Whit clomped down the stairs into Amo's studio while she worked. "Rug needs cleaning."

Her thought suspended in her fingertips over the keys, Amo said, "I'll do it later on."

"It's dirty now."

"It's probably been dirty for two and a half days and you haven't noticed." Amo sighed.

"Do it now!" said Whit.

"I'm working," Amo said calmly. "I'll do it *today*, but later."

"When I say this doctor's office is dirty, you clean it," Whit said, stonefaced with tension.

Amo frowned, shocked.

"You think you're getting a free ride," he raged, "that you can sit there . . . and daydream."

"You heard the typewriter. That's why you came down—to stop me."

"Don't you think *I'd* be a writer if I had the time?" Whitney's tone got bitter, nasty. "If I could sit on my duff and dream up situations. . . . I hardly have time to work on my paper for the seminar."

"Then why did you become a doctor?" asked Amo.

"I had people to support." That cold righteous face accused her of heat, excess, heedlessness.

"Not when you got your MD," said Amo, "not till you *chose* to marry. If you'd really wanted to be a writer, you would've made it possible for yourself. At least, you would've written more than one paper."

Webb spun around, charged upstairs to his desk, charged back down. "Here," he slung the seminar paper at her. "This time I want you to read it *carefully* and edit it for me."

The phone rang. "Dr. Webb," he barked. It was for Amo. "A man's voice," he said.

"Hello. . . . Evan! Jesus, honey, what are you doing in town? . . . Great, I'll watch the show. I saw the reviews. . . . Um, I don't know, Evan. Hold on." Amo put her hand over the mouthpiece. "Can I meet a writer friend, Evan Connell from San Francisco, for a drink?"

"Why don't you ask him to come here at nine, to see us both?"

She did. He couldn't. "I'd love to see you, Evan, but I guess I can't, if you can't make it by here. . . . Yeah, it *is* silly. I'm sorry. . . . Have fun in town. Maybe next time. . . . So long, Evan."

Whit smiled. "Now, there, that was painless, wasn't it?"

Suddenly Amo remembered the D.O.D. with tenderness, and wondered how she'd strayed so far away from home. She felt really down.

The front door slammed and Whit ran upstairs to see his next patient.

"Ruth, dear," Amo heard him say. Once more he was with company and she was alone.

The paper was for the existential seminar at the Institute. Since the analysts were innocent of the history and literature of Western culture, the seminar hoped to correct that premed educational oversight. Hence, budding thirty-five-year-old analysts were forever coming up with some brilliant insight that abounded in undergraduate schools throughout the land. That there were valid ideas in fiction seemed especially suspect, hardly creditable unless subsumed into the mess kit of psychological theory.

Whit's paper stirred up the topics of passion and boredom in the modern novel. One idea did strike Amo. She edited it to read:

> The real Nothingness is Possessiveness because then the person is so involved in pleasing and fearing the Other, and demanding that the Other please him, that he forgets his own identity, loses the ability to see what his own desires are and hence cannot please himself. The self shrinks, shrivels. . . .

"You wrote those lines," she said to Whit later. "Did you mean them?"

He seethed. "What else? Did you edit it?"

"Can't you tell?"

"No."

"Only that page. I don't see any point till you

rewrite it. Instead of Flaubert and Goncharov, why don't you use Nabokov and Doris Lessing?" Amo suggested. "Everybody knows boredom replaces passion in monogamy today. Passion is not just a state, but dependent on circumstances such as novelty, detail, spring, etc." She said all this as if it had no relation to them.

Whit stood there rocking on his heels. "Anything else, Mom?"

"Don't convolute your sentences so much—be simpler and colorful."

He gave her a look of zealous hatred. "Just as you say."

"Whit, you asked me for criticism, didn't you?"

"Not a demolition job," he said, and stomped upstairs.

"You can't expect your first effort—"

But he was gone, up to the waiting live body who didn't criticize, who only obeyed or intended to, Daddy, who lusted after submission to his superior will. His protective arms. Whitney often felt his arms were like protective antennae, a web covering the city that all his patients, now and before and evermore, clung to. Some swung loose, some clutched, some nuzzled up into his armpit, others seemed to let go, but few actually did. It was a form of love, their offering to him.

"Hello, Eric." He nodded curtly, comforting both Eric and himself. Eric had been with him six years.

Whit's mother, Simone, phoned back. "If you decide to come Sunday dinner is at seven-thirty."

"Once more, Simone—no. Is that clear?" Whit slammed the phone down.

Eric began his familiar homosexual plaint and Whit switched his mind into Drone & Lull. Some of the patients' monologues were quite soothing. Unlike the prying wheedling voice of his mother who tried to control him, or his bitch of a wife who'd done the same. Only now Chelo was trying to destroy him, ruin his career, in spite of the alimony and child support she got off it. Anything to keep him away from his son, Adam. Chelo had even tried to get his own mother and several local analysts to help her have Whit institutionalized as mentally unstable. His own mother had *listened*; Simone the bitch had *discussed* it with Chelo. He'd never forgive her for that.

"You don't want to sleep with your mother. You want to kill her," Amo had said once, joking. True, true. He told Adam his mother, Chelo, was a bitch, and Adam slapped him. He wanted Adam to know he had an alternative—his father. Well, Adam didn't understand yet, at eight. But the seed had been planted; he'd sprinkle it now and then.

What was Eric saying? Webb widened his eyes and nodded sagely. Where was he? Adam. Yes, Adam was too young to listen. Chelo refused to. Now Amo was acting up. At least she wasn't a clinger like Beverly and Marta, the concert painist, who'd preceded her. He'd turned around some emasculating patients and made them into real women, but it wasn't so easy in your personal life. People resisted out of spite. Take his bitch mother, Simone, the writer, the renowned critic, who'd turned his father into a dead alcoholic by age forty-two. He'd shown Amo his father's unpublished novel and Amo was polite; shit, condescending. Too much of the Southern lady Judge in her. Whit knew the novel was good; it had to be; his father did it.

Eric was getting out of the orange director's chair he liked. Was he finished? The session must be over then. "Till Thursday, Eric," Whit dismissed him and Eric backed out. "About your mother, Eric—all women are shits and bitches. Why don't you tell her so?"

Eric clasped his hands. "Oh, may I, Dr. Webb?"

Whitney nodded profoundly.

Eric sashayed out, hips swinging wildly, grinning from ear to ear. "Hi, sweedie," he called to Amo who was winding down the stairs to her studio. "How's the slave trade?" He seldom saw Amo without an appliance in tow.

"Flourishing, Eric." Amo knew he'd never go straight; what did he come for? He needed a stern attentive parent. All these people who needed the heavy hand. Amo thought it was ridiculous and sad, so sad. So little love in the city and each blaming himself because he couldn't get any.

Back to the typewriter. Amo didn't know if she was getting into the new novel but God knows she was pushing, prodding, shoving. Today she seemed to ride the invisible beam.

Whitney burst in. "Why don't you have the guts to hate your mother?" he enquired.

Amo's arms dropped. "Why should I?" said Amo, assuming he meant her Earthmother, the Judge.

"Look what she did to you."

Amo sighed heavily. "Jesus H., what now?"

Whit trained his professional eyes on her psyche. "She made you suppress your natural loving feminine nature—which you had to do to fight her—and turn to fantasy, to writing, for compensation. She made you into a detached person who can't comply with love."

Amo was confused. "Who—you or me?"

"*I'm* willing. Name your terms," Whit smiled frigidly.

"Whitney, I wish you wouldn't invade my studio when I'm working—*please!*"

"Who's paying for it?"

"I am," said Amo, "with housework, cooking, washing, cleaning—"

"Then do it,"—Whit pointed up to the waiting room where, once again, the gold rug was dirtying hourly,—"*now.*" He grabbed her arm and tugged her toward the stairs.

Amo slapped him brushingly, almost playfully, and Whit slapped her back so hard her head spun.

"Think about that for awhile," the Doctor said and mounted the stairs.

Rubbing her face, she did. Though humiliated, she was still Maruvian and concerned about him. Had she not meant to be mean, hiding in playfulness? Perhaps so. He always ferreted out her ultimate motive, or at least her worst. But what about Whit? He seemed to project a load of psychic baggage onto her and expect her to carry it—all these bedtime stories for impotent little boys about mammoth bitch women who seemed to be everywhere, versus feminine butterfly women who seemed to have died off.

Did Amo disqualify as a mistress, a lovable househump? A househump merited love because she served, sewed on buttons, didn't attempt transcendence, always managed to be weaker than the dumptruck she lived with. Whit would claim she dominates the home; she doesn't dominate herself; all he has to do is take the dumptruck away.

Submissiveness pays off, Amo; you know that. How she longed to talk to W.R. instead of herself. You want to turn this menage into marriage? Be a secretary, a stew, a nurse, or a model who means it—helpmeet to that fully human being, the Man. Whit the Man, the you-man being, the hoohoohawhaw. . . . Househumps and dumptrucks deserve each other.

Amo couldn't stand being punished for being an Outsider, for not being inferior. Amo couldn't stand serving an Earthman. "Anything else, honey?" she said at dinner, at breakfast, twenty times a day. But she did it.

This unconscious Gobbler who oppressed her, did she really love him—glom him, whatever you call it—because she had to glom to survive? Because no one but he—in order to do her in—had offered her glom. So-called Lasting Glom, that wouldn't evaporate with the dew in a month or two but continue for maybe a couple of years.

Chapter 27
Theoretical Hi-Jinks

Into the breach stepped Whitney with a theory for Amo's feelings of oppression.

Good = Oppression
Bad = Freedom

Whit said this explained Amo's psyche. With the modeling, she oppressed herself by being a tableau of male desire, the adult equivalent of the good little girl sitting quietly with a bow in her hair. With the writing, it was the same—she felt oppressed by it because she thought it was a *good* thing to do. Therefore, she hated it and had a hard time doing it, succeeding with it.

"Who," said Amo, "me or you? I get high off it, not to mention horny. I've had two offers."

Whit lowered his smooth-brained forehead till his eyes were aimed at her dead level. "You protest too much—trying to be *good* again."

"Bullshit," said Amo. "I *do* the work— you don't."

"You're not the first artist I've treated . . . known."

A flush went over Webb.

Amo snickered.

"Sorry. Habit."

"Don't you mean convicted?"

Whit cleared his throat. "You think creating is hard work, and you torment—oppress yourself with it."

Amo trilled with laughter. '"*You*—or me? Whit, you shouldn't force yourself to write just because your mother is good at it and your father wasn't."

Whit blinked in astonishment.

"It has to be *your* thing—you have to love the involvement." He looked so mortified, so exposed, that she added, "If I believed your terminology, which I don't, I could say you want to beat your mother at her own game in order to destroy her and vindicate your father, that you feel this as an oppressive duty owed your dead father in the name of masculinity for you both."

Webb left the studio in a stoneblind rage.

Amo stood there worried, wondering whether to call W.R. for advice.

Suddenly Whit reappeared, smiling smoothly. "Since you only feel *free* when you're being bad," he went on, "I'm afraid you'll fall in the sack with someone else, to feel, quote, free."

"Bad?"

"Let me explain," said Daddy. "Since being good makes you feel oppressed, you feel confined and you blame it on me. Then you want to break free by punishing me, by being destructive, and so you sleep with another man."

"Witless, I only wanted to have a drink with Evan."

"Who?"

"Evan, the writer."

"You thought I was thinking of him?" Whit snickered. "How petty."

Amo approached Whit and put her arms around his neck into the soft hair at the back. "Honey, do we have to do this?"

He turned his head aside, silky blond and sour.

"Let's go up to the waiting . . . living room." It was Sunday, the only day they could sit in the luxurious stage set for the patients. On Saturday Whit brought Adam to the house, so Amo had to get out. Whit's lawyer said that "Adam could not be introduced to a criminal relationship," as adultery was considered even with a legal separation, and therefore "Adam should not see or know of the existence of your mistress." Only once, when Amo was silently upstairs, did she see the blond head and tiny body from the back as they went to Whit's car, a red Maserati. Amo felt left out. She'd looked forward to mothering Adam once a week.

They went up to the fancy sofas and gold carpet and elegant fireplaces, and sat. No TV or record player, no café table or kitchen or studio—barren up here. They couldn't see the folks passing outside because the windows were just that much above street level. But they could watch windows across the way, infinitely finer windows than on West Fifty-funky.

"A perfect example," Whit's arm indicated the ceiling. "You refuse to clean the chandeliers. You know why? Because it oppresses you to be good. That would be pleasing me,"—his tone nagged with petulance—"and you wouldn't dream of that, would you, Miss Inspired Tidbit, Miss Genius of the Month."

"Why in shit should I clean six hundred bitsy pieces of glass?" Amo hollered.

"Because it's your fucking job in this house," Whit roared.

Amo bellowed so loud her throat felt sore, "I'd rather be a whore than a goddamn cleaning woman."

"Who says you're not?" Whit detonated the silent splendor. "My convenient little piece of ass, you stupid cunt." He stood over her, squeezing her arms like a vice. "If she doesn't shut her fucking mouth, I'm going to beat her to a bloody pulp."

Chapter 28
Offers

W.R. was not all that eager to talk to Amo when she called. She signaled for half an hour before he deigned to reply. Understandably.

W.R. (harshly): "The only good thing you've done recently was to turn down Foxy."

AMO: "Thanks, W.R." (Nostalgically) "How are things spinning? How's everybody? I feel so out of touch."

W.R.: "Smoothly, A.M.O., though—"

AMO: "I've missed you, W.R., so much."

W.R.: "Yes . . . yes, so have I. It hasn't been the same at this old way station."

AMO: "Here, either."

W.R. (dismayed): "What on Earth has happened to you, A.M.O.?"

AMO: "Co-opted out."

W.R. (buzzing silence): "You seem . . . weak, very weak,"

AMO: "It's awful depending on someone who can throw you out if you don't please him."

W.R.: "You *know* they love off their ego, A.M.O.

Every Maruvian schoolchild learns about the easily structured Earth mind—little cellular cubicles waiting to be plugged with jargon—"

AMO: "—unctuous for definition. That's the human form of peace on Earth, W.R. Define it, and they relax. The Oedipus complex justifies the male ego which justifies male bonding which justifies territorial war. Or put another way: masters manipulate men—men manipulate women—women manipulate children—children behead cats to learn to be men, tear up dolls to learn to be women."

W.R.: "The old primordial power play, A.M.O."

AMO: "What do you think of his theory?"

W.R.: "*You* and *I* think oppression is bad and freedom is good. But you're not acting like it. Why don't you leave him?"

AMO; "Because he offered me love. I know there are better men to love, W.R., but nobody offers much . . . these days . . . on Earth. I think he wants to love me, if he can."

W.R. (despairing): "Oh, A.M.O. Can't you be less Maruvian and more of an egotist?"

AMO: "But I know how frightened he is."

W.R.: "I don't think that's going to save you."

AMO: "What do you mean by that?"

W.R.: "Most murderers are frightened people."

AMO: "Oh, really, W.R." She cut him off with a snap of her wrist.

Chapter 29
Children

"Remember the Primal Scene?" Steve Luks chortled.

"I said I dreamt it," said Whit.

"I said I saw it—in Technicolor," said Luks.

"What?" Amo asked.

"My parents having sex—that's the Primal Scene," said Whit. "Sets up the infantile complexes."

"Absolutely essential," Steve winked at Amo. "Can't advance to the next class level till you admit it." Steve was one of the few analysts she'd met through Whit who didn't seem afraid of women.

Amo snortled, Whit frowned.

"Now I remember," Amo jiggled with laughter. "Clomped together they were, and I got into the middle of the sandwich and they both ate me up. Pardon me, she did!"

Steve hollered, Whitney looked pale. Beside Whit, Dr. Stefan Luks appeared to be a furry beaver with Gypsy eyes and castanet. Beside Steve, Whit looked like a tall Brahmin with the gangling washed-out quality of the overbred. Tonight they had drinks in the underground cave studio. Tomorrow Amo and Whit would be in Court and there would be no more laughter.

Amo excused herself because she had a problem of her own to consider.

"I'm pregnant," Amo said to the Wrist Radar.

W.R.: "Take a Tasty."

AMO: "They don't have Tasties here. I have to get it cut out or vacuumed out."

W.R.: "How primitive! By whom?"

AMO: "Doctors—MD's."

W.R.:"What about the one you live with?"

AMO: "I haven't told him yet—because I think I want to have it."

W.R. (rumbling): "Because your book wasn't bought?"

AMO: "Probably."

W.R.: "A baby for a book—a real cop-out."

AMO (discouraged, admitting it): "Yep. I've had it, W.R."

W.R.: "You're not married. You have no money. Why can't you abide by the rules down there?"

AMO: "They're not *like* ours. Justice is only a concept—it's never practiced. I've had two illegal abortions, W.R. I think it's time I had an Earthchild."

W.R. (sadly): "But then you *will* get married, and you'll never come back."

AMO (impatiently): "Does everything have to be so tragic to you, W.R.? I'll be back. It only takes twenty years to raise a child."

W.R.: "What makes you so sure Webb wants it?
Suppose he doesn't? What then?"

Last week Amo had her key in the entrance door,
other arm toting groceries, when a man called out, "Hi
there, Amo." She turned smiling and he stuck the
subpoena in her coat pocket, saying, "Okay, it touched
you. You're served."

Amo flipped the envelope out of her pocket, threw it
at the man, and whipped into the house, locking the
door behind her.

The man tossed it in the mail slot, shouting, "I said
you're served, sister."

She threw it out the slot. He threw it back in. Amo
was served, all right.

Chelo's lawyer subpoenaed her as a witness for their
side, for Chelo's contention that Whitney was an unfit
parent and should not be allowed to see their son,
Adam, at all, ever. Apparently Whit's lack of fitness
was partially due to his living in open adultery with
Amo. Whit was countersuing Chelo for denying him
visitation rights on his designated Saturdays, claiming
she was an unfit mother.

"If we don't get Judge Bardetta, the sex fiend, we'll
be all right," said Whit's lawyer, Josh Heilmann,
pushing back his mop of gray hair.

Amo dressed as Miss Prim & Grim, per instructions.

"What an unappetizing woman," Josh said happily
when he saw her in black dress, hair skimmed back.

If the Judge found out Amo had been a nude model,

Josh warned, it could destroy Whit's case. To Amo, the story they'd concocted for her seemed childish and unbelievable. But she knew Whitney would never forgive her if he lost the right to see his son because *she* fouled up. Amo hoped it united them—a common enemy.

"Oh, my God!" said Josh when he saw the docket.

They entered Judge Bardetta's courtroom. White-haired, sour-visaged, bleary-eyed with boredom, that's how Bardetta looked to Amo—a sort of saggy elder bureaucrat.

A pretty young Puerto Rican woman joined them.

"Is that Chelo?" Amo asked Whit.

He blushed. "No, that's the maid."

Then a fat little bug lady came in, a bluebottle with huge eyes and three chins, standing 4' 11" in spike heels and eyeliner.

"That's Chelo."

Wads of fat slanted down her back under the cerise suit. Black stringy hair spilled out under the pillbox hat and veil. Whit whispered that she must've put on thirty pounds in the past year. Amo was horrified because Chelo's degeneration showed so clearly how unhappy she was, how she hated herself, life, Whit, the world.

The Judge swore them in, contestants and witnesses both. The maid had been called by Whit's side to show that Chelo mistreated Adam. Then there was an MD called by Chelo's side to show that Adam suffered anxiety when faced with his father. Adam himself was nowhere in sight.

As a witness, Amo had to wait outside with the others in the drafty corridors till her turn came. For Whitney's sake, she had to do well. The doctor sweated and concentrated just as she did, both rehearsing their phony stories.

Chapter 30
Hyah Come De Judge

Amo was sworn in, gave her name and address, and sat in the witness chair. She tried to smile at Whit and Josh.

Chelo's lawyer was Herman Lamb—large and soft, 6'4" with dewlaps. Lamb got right to it. "Isn't it true that you live at that address with Dr. Webb?"

AMO: "Not exactly."

LAMB: "Isn't it true that you left your apartment and your job to move in with Dr. Webb?"

AMO (breathing deeply): "Well, Dr. Webb offered me work and I was looking for a nicer place to live, so I came here and rented a room from the Doctor." Amo blanched; who could believe such guff?

LAMB: "What sort of job did you have?"

AMO: "I'm a fiction writer. My agent is sending my novel around to publishers."

LAMB: "Have you ever had anything published?"

AMO: "Several short stories."

LAMB: "But never a novel?"

AMO: "Not yet."

The Judge interrupted, waving it all away. "Oh,

you'll probably never get it published. Everybody writes novels." He looked at her closely.

AMO (trying to be friendly): "It's difficult, but I've had two—"

JUDGE BARDETTA: "Did I ask for your comments?" He looked at her even more closely. A familiar face the young woman had, beneath the modest disguise.

AMO: "But, I—"

JUDGE (hostile): *"Did* I ask for your comments?"

AMO: "No. . . . "

JUDGE: "Then don't interrupt. Confine your opinions to yourself and answer the questions." He gave her a hysterical Fundamentalist eye, which was followed by a strange smirk. He had recognized Amo.

AMO (submissive and polite, as she'd been instructed): "Yes."

LAMB: "Did you make a living from your writing?"

AMO: "No—my family helped me out."

LAMB: "I thought you had a job."

AMO: "Not a regular job." Amo glanced at Whit, who watched intently.

LAMB: "What kind of job?"

AMO: "I did TV commercials and product demonstrations at trade shows." Indeed, she had.

The Judge's snake smirk was trained on Amo. The slut was trying to take him in, as if she were invisible in clothes. He knew what she was like in every salacious detail, from those filthy poses in *Meat* when she'd been Tidbit, from *Bachelor's Pad* and *Punt* and *Fleshpot.* He must have twenty magazines with shots of Amo Coove.

LAMB: "Where do you stay in Dr. Webb's house?"

AMO: "I have the upstairs bedroom."

LAMB: "Dr. Webb stays there with you?"

AMO: "No, sir. Dr. Webb sleeps downstairs in the basement."

LAMB: "You *do* have sexual intercourse with Dr. Webb?"

AMO (gulping): "Yes, sir."

LAMB: (laughing): "And you expect me to believe you sleep upstairs and he down?"

AMO (swooning with the inanity of all this): "We felt it was more proper that way."

LAMB: "Proper? Do you have intercourse every day?"

AMO: "What gall!" She looked to Whit and Josh for help. Josh shook his head once, meaning play it straight.

JUDGE BARDETTA: "Answer the question, missy." He glowered down at her from his vulture's perch.

AMO: "Not so often. Intermittently."

LAMB: "But living in the same house makes it easier to have sexual intercourse?"

AMO: "Not necessarily."

LAMB: "More convenient, then?"

AMO: "Convenient? I came here because I love Dr. Webb and we hope to be legally married as soon as possible."

JUDGE (angrily shouting): "It makes it easier to have sexual intercourse, doesn't it?"

AMO: "Anybody can have sex. It's love that's rare. That's why I came here." She blinked at Whitney.

JUDGE (about to explode, leaning over the podium toward Amo): "Answer the question! It's easier to have sex if you live together—isn't it, isn't it?"

AMO: "Yes."

JUDGE (glowering): "Then don't try to deny it, you—" One more evasion and he'd let the tart have it. He remembered the famous color shot of her on her hands and knees, that monstrous bosom hanging down. What was it in? Oh, yes, that little booklet called *All About Amo*.

LAMB: "Dr. Webb supports you?"

AMO: "I work for him as an editorial secretary. I keep the patients' records and help him with scientific articles."

LAMB: "Have you ever done scientific writing?"

AMO: "No, but I know something about style and clarification of ideas."

LAMB: "Have you ever written scientific articles?"

AMO: "No."

Lamb exchanged amused glances with Judge Bardetta. He went on to ask if Amo had ever seen Adam—No—and if she left clothes or pictures where he might see them—No—then to what he considered the coup. "Do you have friends in L.A.?"

AMO: "Doesn't everybody?"

LAMB: "Do you know Malachi Stein?"

AMO (surprised): "Yes."

Lamb showed Amo an envelope addressed to Mrs. Whitney Webb which had evidently been sent on to Chelo. Inside was a congratulations card and a note saying: "There are only three constants in life—death, money, and change."

LAMB: "Is this his handwriting?"

AMO: "Seems to be."

LAMB: "He addresses you as Mrs. Whitney Webb."

AMO: "I haven't seen him in a long time. He probably just assumes—"

JUDGE (loudly): "Stop making comments! He said he addressed you as Mrs. Whitney Webb. Did he or didn't he?"

AMO: "Apparently he did, but—"

JUDGE: "All right! That's all you were asked."

LAMB: "So you passed yourself off publicly as Mrs. Whitney Webb?"

AMO: "I didn't—not to anybody!"

LAMB (with a flourish): "He addresses you as Mrs. Webb. I think that's sufficient. That's all."

Dazed, wanting to explain further, Amo rose to go.

LAMB: "Don't you want your mail?"

Amo took the envelope and stepped down, glancing at Whit and Josh's unreadable faces, wondering if beneath the grim exterior Chelo was chuckling inside. Probably not. Amo was sent out of the room.

The doctor followed Amo onstage to talk about Adam's anxiety in relation to his father's weekly visits. They broke for lunch. Josh, with his gray tousled hair and blithe energy, didn't seem too worried, but he was worried. After lunch the maid testified that Chelo often ignored both children and sometimes slapped Adam without cause. Another witness, a woman, testified that Chelo worked part-time with her selling real estate even though she received alimony and child support. All of this apparently bored the Judge.

Toward the end of the afternoon, Amo snuck into

the courtroom and sat in the back row. The Judge appeared to be delivering Fundamentalist sermons to the wall above her head, talking to himself, gesticulating, chuckling, growling. He didn't seem to hear the lawyers at all. Amo wondered if he could see her. She watched Chelo. From Whit's tales, she'd expected to hate Chelo. But the first sight of Chelo's upholstered despair changed that.

The Judge threw out the contempt case against Chelo and returned to the area that kept him awake. He glowered at all his subjects down below and said from the bench, "Well, these people *say* there's been no exposure of the child. But they're evidently sex-crazed and I can't trust Dr. Webb or this common tramp he lives with. They're liable one day to let their emotions run away with them and have sexual intercourse in front of the child."

Shock kept the entire courtroom silent. Then Josh slammed some papers down on the table.

The Judge ignored that and looked about blindly. "Get that missy up here so she'll hear me good—that Amo Coove."

Amo walked forward slowly, beginning to understand, till she stood next to the table where Whit and Josh sat.

"All right, you two—" Perversity most foul was implied, as the Judge laid his bleary smirk on Amo. "This stinking situation—this so-called relationship —must be terminated because the atmosphere is contaminating the child. My decision about ceasing Dr. Webb's visitation rights with his son will be held over till Monday and will depend on the adulterous relationship ending." The mallet bonked and the Judge gathered himself for his departure.

All the principals looked at one another. Josh stepped up to Judge Bardetta and spoke quietly, gesturing wildly, came back slumped. Amo looked at Chelo who was too clever to smile.

"What does he mean?" Amo asked Josh. Josh herded them out of the courtroom, away from the opposition, before he said, "He means you can't live together anymore."

Amo looked to Whit. "Josh, you mean we have to *pretend* to break up."

"No—for real," said Josh, turning to Whit. "You heard him—he's crazy, senile! If you live together he'll keep you from ever seeing Adam again. He's done it before."

Whitney drove home, stonefaced. Amo's eyes never left him. "What are we going to do, Whit?"

"You heard Josh."

"I won't go."

They went into the house. Whit greeted a matronly patient in the subdued tone he sometimes affected and released his arm from Amo's grip. "We can't discuss it now."

Amo trembled. "This is my home twenty-four hours a day, and I'm not leaving so you can see that sacred son four hours on Saturday." She raced upstairs wailing and slammed the bedroom door, leaving Whit and the patient blushing at her unseemly rage.

Whit turned to his patient. "That's what *you* have to learn to do, Sylvia."

Chapter 31
Blocking

After his last patient, Whit clomped down to the studio cave where Amo sipped tequila, feet up on the cocktail table, tamping down her dread with cactus juice. If only she had some grass to ease the fear of losing him, lessen the caring. Stubbornly, she had not called W.R.

"Probably would've broken up anyway,"—Whit carefully mixed a margarita—"because of our sex problems."

Always the hand of threat poked into her gut, her blooming gut. "Whitney, are you listening? I'm pregnant."

"Since this morning?"

"I've known for two weeks but I didn't want to upset you before the trial."

"That was good of you," he sipped sarcastically.

"Yes, it was."

"We'll get you an abortion. Probably I can even do it." The urge to tinker with bodies rather than heads came over him, to balance again those delicate steel tools. As an intern he'd delivered babies, sutured stab wounds, led an exciting TV life. "Did I ever tell you how much fun it was to hang around the hospital? Even on days off, it was our corner bar, midnight drugstore."

"It's nice to have that—a place." She shook her head. "That's why I want to have the baby, Whit. You and me and the baby—that's a place."

"Why lay this on me? I've got one—two, that is."

"You don't want it?" she said helplessly. "It's ours—our own."

He threw his head back and laughed, then leveled his eyes on her the way he did with his mother. "Don't expect me to accept inauthentic pseudo-love just because you're pregnant." The analysts were winding through Sartre and Heidegger and Authenticity at their meetings.

"Pseudo?" she blinked. "What do you mean, our sex problems? I thought I'd learned to do it your way."

"That's what I mean," he glinted triumphantly. "You're faking it."

"Faking? Here, I'll show you whether I'm faking." Amo slung her arms around his neck and planted a brimming kiss on him.

"You kissed me right that time." Whit pulled away. "Now, try it again."

She did.

"Nope, it's gone. I knew it would be." Whit shook his head sadly. "I always kiss you the same way— openly—but you, you're a taker."

He kissed her smoothly to try it again and Amo hungrily reached for more. His mouth felt like a cushy pillow with a man hiding behind it, evading contact. He left her with the sucking flab—it sucks her, she sucks it. When she tried to feel more Whit, he pulled away.

"We don't fit," said Whitney. "I'm an oven—you're a furnace. You burn and destroy—"

"You bake for six hours and everybody goes to sleep."

"Maybe you're just too hot for me."

"And you're not aggressive enough for me." Her hands went to her breasts protectively because her breasts were afraid of him. "From the neck up and the waist down." She chuckled at the ridiculous disparity and nuzzled his ear. He was like an insane foreign policy—attack here, don't touch there, don't ask why. "Let's go to bed." Sex talk, good or bad, made Amo hot.

In fact, all their niggling psychological fencing excited her, now that she knew he would always insist on confronting life that way. Like many Earthwomen, Amo was good at using the means available for passion, though she would never have chosen them. Not that she paid much attention to the subject matter, since she could not confine her mind to these equal and opposite grooves he was so fond of.

"Are you sure you want to?" Whit scowled, perplexed.

"Positive, hotshot. Git up those stairs." Amo tried to tease him into dropping the threat of sexual failure, kill loss with laughter and gaiety.

"What did you call me?"

Amo leapt up the stairs and collapsed languorously on the velvet couch in the living/waiting room.

Whit ignored her and trudged up to the bedroom, undoing his tie. She followed and bit him lightly on the fanny as he dropped his pants. "Solemn ass," she said, slinging her clothes off.

"You lack dignity," said Whit.

"Riiiiight." As soon as he was undressed, Amo shifted around to the sixty-nine position and began licking him. "My banana split, my dollop, yum, yum." She crooned, holding it as if it were a mike, "My 'dorable dangle, my poifect prongaling." She swallowed it to halfway, then more, then gagged and settled for halfway. After awhile it became obvious he would not reciprocate. Amo looked up at him, holding her mike, "What's happening up there, sir? I spot a fellow who's not too busy."

"Why don't we start at the beginning?" said Whitney.

"A, B, C, D," said Amo under her breath as she switched around.

Lips to breasts to navel to fringes of the vulva, a nuzzling of the feathers without really touching the nest. Amo figured he would hold out on her since he always carefully paid her back, but she wanted him so much it hardly mattered, so much that she undulated and contracted in bliss till he said, "Stop that. Stop taking. You're supposed to give. I'll set the rhythm." He did, and in no time Amo suck/sank to a percussive orgasm that amplified and echoed through their caresses like warm honey feeding starved veins and cranky muscles. Not long after, Whit pulled out and rolled over onto his back.

Amo cuddled around him, kissing his cheek. "Oh, that felt glorious. I had an orgasm, did you?"

"How could I?" Whit pulled away and sat up. "You were too self-involved. You didn't say *I* felt so good you had an orgasm."

"I *meant* that."

"You used me to jack off, as usual."

She tittered anxiously, "What on Earth do you mean?"

"You interiorized your feelings, just like Chelo used to do. You were not responding to *me*. The best proof of that is that I couldn't *feel* you. If I had been able to feel you, I would've had an orgasm." His face was pale, officious, intensely angry.

"But I—"

"*You* had an orgasm because *I* communicated to you, I *responded* to you. I was open, but you didn't return the favor."

"If I'd been any hotter—" She felt herself, warm and liquefying.

"You're stuck in a self-contained will, like most of the women I've known." He laid the blue preacher's eyes on her. "You all pretend at first, then you revert—to selfishness. You don't let it out."

"I came!"

He jumped up furiously. "I *explained* the reason for that."

Amo shook the tangles from her brain. "Whit, do we have to do this?"

"What, Miss Tidbit?" Whit said, cranky and petulant. "Do I have to accept your phony love and your idiot child and your version of life? You want a rich doctor, kid? Sure, you do. You all do. Try to get him." He hollered with laughter.

"Why don't you go straight and turn queer?" Amo said in disgust.

"Hahaha, she's really down, isn't she?" Whit swung around. "And when she leaves this house, I'm going to sleep with other women and there won't be anything she can do about it."

Tears welled out of Amo's eyes. He so shrilly wanted to do her in. "Don't." She rolled over onto her stomach.

"You don't want me to sleep with other women, do you?" He flipped her over and straddled her, large dog over small cat.

"No," she whispered.

"It upsets you?"

"Yes."

"I'm going to do it anyway and you can't stop me," he threatened.

She shrugged, head turned away from him, wishing he'd move.

"You accept it?"

"What can I do?" she said helplessly. She felt something hard against her leg, much harder than usual.

With a muscular look of Teutonic mastery, he plunged his penis into her. He could really get it up when he'd gotten her down.

Amo made a mistake. She bolted with laughter and his hard-on collapsed. Bolted with the plastic disillusioned laughter of one good at ego games who loathed playing them, whose soul was slowly starving to death, who yet felt responsible to all those people who would not let her touch them.

"I'm sorry." She stroked his hair. "Whit, can't we do it off love instead of hate?"

"Speak for yourself, bitch." He put on a ribbed turtleneck and slacks. "I'm going out. By the way, Josh wants you out of here by Monday."

". . . Monday?"

"If he says you're gone, the Judge won't have an excuse to keep me from Adam."

"I thought we were . . . committed," Amo blubbered.

That sent Whit into gales of laughter. He sobered instantly and said, "You better think about that abortion because I'm not going to be responsible for another child."

"I've got to have someone to love."

"Pretty cliché, Amo."

"Like you do." She glanced around the familiar room, at the habitual man. "I don't want to go."

Whit smiled impatiently. "But you must."

"Where?"

"Where do you usually go?"

Chapter 32
Hug

Whit hadn't branded it on her forehead but Amo knew it was over. A for adultery, A for abortion, A for Amo alone once more. She couldn't bear to be alone again in another furnished room—white cliffs of walls giving her back blankness, no sounds, no eyes, no feet on stairs, no warmth to lean against, no one to scream at from the cornerstone of self erected by the screaming.

This time she'd disappear into the walls if she didn't have a human cry to wake her. Back to the filthy business of exposing herself like a white cliff, like a slab of white meat for the camera. A perfect preservation that lived inside the penny-arcade machine on the Great White Way, miniature, silent, and emerged with the tinkle of coin into living squirming flesh—vanilla hair, pink nips, rose lips, blue bead curtain, purple velvet shoes—teasing, 'ticing, more than humanly On, 'dorable till the sale was over. Back to the box.

(A)tlanta (M)unicipal (O)rphanage—their joke, she and her mother, but Amo remembered the long year she'd spent there before her mother found her—a year of cliff walls and slabs of cots and kids like lone plants reaching for the sun, always reaching, vying for attention, dozens of arms waving toward one disappearing adult.

Then the few years with her mother—two, only, before college—then the wandering adventures, then finally two years with Malachi and now one year with Whitney. All her relationships with people seemed tenuous, as if she begged them to let her stay in the presence of life and they said no. No, sorry, you're . . . isolate.

Something about her didn't fit, except in Maruvia. She watched couples sashay down the block and wondered what it was she didn't do, couldn't sustain. Always, everywhere, she watched couples lean together, fitting, she with her interplanetary eyes. She should never have left Maruvia. She was too old for this place. Outside she was thirty-one, from the Time Stopping Pill, but inside she was forty-six. Her first thirty years—looking fifteen—on Maruvia she was a crime-fighting idealist who operated comfortably alone. Even here on Earth till several years ago it didn't bother her that in all that time she'd only lived five years with people. Till the desert crept inside and took over.

Now she oppressed herself; she loathed her own presence. She only liked other people. She had lost interest in herself so totally that without the child, she was afraid she'd die. She might stop eating and stay in bed, or walk off a subway platform, into a bus at the intersection.

Whitney was so surrounded by life he didn't know what she meant. Even now, he was with a patient. He was talking, communicating, relating. He lived in a web of life—patients, Institute, meetings, colleagues, hospital, sacred son, ex-wife, mother, new woman when he chose.

All Whit had to do was crook his little finger at her replacement. Amo had to sit and wait for the crooking of someone else's finger. Mostly the finger went up inside her, explored, and left.

Probably she didn't offer much. She was not young, docile, rich or famous, neither a househump nor a claqueur. Well, W.R. had warned her. Suddenly Amo wished she had women friends, but she never had. Women didn't like her because of her Nudie business and she didn't like the other models because they were money-huggers and narcs (narcissists). Then too she'd been so busy with men, hunting a mate. Or idealizing with W.R.

Whit entered the bedroom and made a noise of disgust at Amo's tear-stained face. He gargled before the next patient and said, "When Simone comes by, don't mention any of this."

"Of course not." Amo sat up, staving off rejection. "Whit, the important thing is how we feel about each other, whether we care enough to make it together. Do you?" She reached for him.

·Whit backed away. "I've told you before. I love you but you're faking it." Whit laid a lingering eye on her then wheeled out, down the stairs to greet a new customer.

Amo crumbled into raging tears. She went into the

bathroom so the holy seer's patients couldn't hear her. She turned the basin faucets on full blast and jumped into the bathtub. She lay in the tub cuddled up on her side cowering, screaming with sobs, so loud she had to cover her own ears. There was nothing she could do, she couldn't reach him—nothing at all.

Whit's mother, Simone, came for a drink on Amo's invitation, not Whit's. Simone was a friendly gray behemoth with a cane, in her shaggy sixties. She wore a large floppy plum velvet hat and beaded choker and a caftan. Amo knew why aging creative women dressed bizarre—it was better than looking decrepit. Amo and Simone liked each other, having much in common, including loneliness.

"My dear, I liked those two chapters immensely," Simone said with lectern presence. "You must give me more—tonight. No excuses."

Amo was pleased. Whit talked stiffly about the trial, revealing nothing, so that when Simone left she was able casually to say, "Be happy, children," and shake the manuscript wickedly at Amo. "I'll let you know."

Amo helped Simone on with her coat. Simone went to kiss her son good-bye but Whit sidled behind Amo, so Simone was forced to kiss Amo only. Amo gave her a good hug because they shared that too—Whit wouldn't let his mother touch him, not even on the arm. Simone's eyes always glazed with sadness but there was nothing she could do. Nothing at all either of them could do, miscast as they were by the blind director.

Chapter 33
Moving Day

Monday morning Amo awoke for the last time in bed with Whit on pleasant East Seventy-sunny. Whit was due in Court at eleven. Before that, he and Steve Luks were helping Amo move back to the West Side into a single room at the D.O.D., the six-by-ten room formerly occupied by the Super, Mr. O'Donovan, who had gone to Bellevue to finish dying of lung cancer. "You're in luck," the managing agent had said when she phoned him Saturday.

Amo reached for Whitney who scooted away and into the bathroom to shower. She felt her stomach, poofing it out as if it were bigger. The desert had sprouted a blossom. How astonishing she could still green with the light. She started weeping again. Other women chose between home and career, and were deprived of one. Amo was deprived of both.

"Get up." Whit tugged at her arm.

Amo tried to, but collapsed into the quilt thrown off the end of the bed on the floor, and clutched it round her, clinging to the nest. She sank into a funk, tingling and prickling all over as if electrodes leaped under her skin, nerves jangled about, power lines crossed and misfired jolts. She was so high with suffering, in such constant intense pain, that she decided she had to end this agony even if she had to kill herself to do it. Anything—death, nothingness—was preferable to this extreme of torture. She tried to reach W.R. but her body static was so loud she couldn't hear him.

Whit and Steve packed the zippy red car with Amo's two bags and café table. The altar desk would be over later. Amo wilted against the congealed city tree in front of the house, almost unable to stand, wanting to lie down right there on the sidewalk. A little friendly bit of dirt and a tree that had been her front yard.

Steve said something to Amo who watched his lips move but couldn't hear him. She teetered there on the edge of collapse, staring down the street at the inside of her agony, not seeing, about to explode like a bomb and only wishing the explosion would take place instead of merely expanding, expanding, aching more and more. Whit came up and took her by the arm and she clutched the tree in a tight embrace.

"Am I going to have to peel you off there?" he asked.

Whit tugged and Amo held on.

People stopped to stare. Whit yanked and Amo's small hands gave way. Half limp, she got into the car. Steve was in the seat in back. Whit locked his seat belt and motioned for Amo to do the same. She elbowed his arm away and they started crosstown.

"The kind Doctor," she hissed, "keep him clean— the mercy man." She wanted to kill him, scrape him, gouge him, rip him, smash him. She wanted to die there on the spot, finish it all, get rid of her suffering abyss of feeling, anyway, anyhow, but now.

They picked up speed crossing the park. Amo opened the car door on her side and jumped. Steve grabbed her left shoulder from behind and jerked her by the armpit back into the car. Amo struggled to leave the car feet first. Pedestrians stared, startled, and wheeled with the car as it careened on. Steve flung Amo over on her stomach and slammed the car door and locked it. He kept his arm on the locked door. Whit reached for Amo.

"What a cheap cunt trick!" Whit said furiously.

"What do you care if I throw myself into the street?" wailed Amo. "You're throwing me there anyway."

Chapter 34
Pfaff

Back in the D.O.D., Amo felt like an escaped prisoner returned to solitary to serve out her life sentence. There were bars on the one window which faced the garbagey court of the building behind. She couldn't walk the length of the room because her altar desk sat flush against the cot. If she stepped down too hard on the mattress, the smell of organic decay hung on the air. She phoned Mr. O'Donovan at Bellevue and he asked her to come visit him.

Simone had invited her in but Whit had said no, that would look like collusion. "Don't try to get at me through Simone," Whit had warned. Amo was back on Death Row, feeling her stomach where the hope was.

The bell rang. She buzzed in Jonelle and her mother, Sarah, who lived across the street, and started down the stairs. "You don't have to come all the way up, Sarah. I'll get her."

"Thanks, Amo. I'll just be a hour," said Sarah and went off to buy groceries.

"Well, angel," said Amo, sitting on the first landing, "let's see you climb."

Jonelle looked like a black Kewpie doll with amazed eyes, full of questions and concerns and two-year-old energy. "Hey, Amo," she said when she reached her lap and sat gazing at her face, inspecting.

They walked up, hand in hand. "What we do today?" Jonelle wagged her Afro and twinked her eyes.

"Oh, I think we'll say words and have art class."

While they said words, Jonelle felt Amo's lips and face and blubbered. She was much better at scribbling.

Webb slit open the letter. ". . . astounding perception . . . brilliant . . . conceived with freewheeling imagination." He grinned from ear to ear, sat back. His first effort accepted by the first psychoanalytic journal he'd sent it to.

He frowned. Pfaff? Who was Pfaff? He sat up and examined the letterhead—Pfaff & Company—then saw it was addressed to Amo's literary agent who had sent the Xerox on to her. It was an offer to buy Amo's novel, signed by—of course—a lady editor. But at the bottom was a note, handwritten: "The most ingenious mythology I've read in years. Polycarp Pfaff, President."

Seething, Whit ripped it to shreds.

The public phone rang on the floor below. Sometimes Amo answered it, sometimes not. It was Whit who said a letter came from her literary agent.

"Read it," Amo said with resignation.

"Can't. I've already forwarded it," said Whit. "Say, I'm going to an Institute forum in Boston over the weekend. Would you like to go?"

"Sure," said Amo, surprised.

"Okay. We'll drive up. Be over here Friday at six PM sharp."

Amo brightened. "Say, that's nice of you, Whit."

"Sure," said Whit, hanging up.

Amo couldn't make herself contact the model agencies, the crummy movie business, the horny amateurs again. Not yet, not till hunger forced it. The room cost $8 a week. She bought a hot plate, and kept her milk and meat in a box on the window ledge. The pigeons snipped at the box with their beaks now and then. The milk was never cold enough.

She visited Mr. O'Donovan, the Super, at Bellevue. He was very thin and distressed and his hands shook.

"Amo, they came in one day and I was crying so they put me in the mental ward. Nobody likes to die, Amo. I told them that but they wouldn't listen." He began crying and she held his hands. "I have to die with the crazies."

Amo told him she liked his room, that it was cozy.

Mr. O'Donovan brightened a bit. "I'm so glad to pass it on to a nice person. It's a friendly little room, isn't it?"

"Do you have relatives?" Amo's eyes misted. "Is somebody taking care of you?"

"My brother and sister-in-law come every day. They've been good." He looked at Amo like a frightened trusting child, his voice a whispery croak. He said very slowly, "Remember when we had that fight about integration . . . and I called you a nigger lover? All my nurses have been black . . . and they've been wonderful to me . . . wonderful. You showed me the light there."

"They did," said Amo, squeezing his old bony dry hands, both of them weeping.

"How's your writing coming, Amo? I always knew you'd have big success there."

Amo lowered her head and shrugged.

Chapter 35
Gouge

There in the double living room Whitney welcomed Amo with a glass of Harvey's Bristol Cream from a decanter on a silver tray. Very genial host, he seemed. Silky hair, smooth eyes, soft lighting and knit body shirt.

Amo glanced up at something sparkling and realized what it was. "The chandeliers are clean."

"The maid did it yesterday," said Whit. "How are you feeling?" He leaned toward her in his analyst's posture, legs apart, elbows on knees, body sympathetically forward.

"Rotten . . . lonely."

"I mean, the pregnancy. How far along are you?"

"About two months, maybe less."

"Seen a doctor?"

"Not since the diagnosis."

"Why don't I examine you to see how you're doing?" He grinned. "A freebie—take advantage." He indicated his dining-table desk which was covered with a mattress and a bedsheet.

It looked like a quack's homemade setup. Amo frowned. "Can you see back there?"

"Sure." Whit whipped on two baby spots especially set up for the occasion.

"Whit, I'm not a guinea pig. Where are your instruments?"

"Right here, m' dear." With another wave of the arm, he indicated a sterile container.

Amo disliked his air of Playing Doctor.

Gently he took her by the arm. "Go to the john now and urinate. Leave your skirt on but remove your underpants, and come out with the sheet around you."

Amo looked at him closely, distrustfully.

"God, Amo, don't you trust me?" Very blue-eyed and blond, he laughed and patted her fanny. "Go along now."

Amo did as instructed and came out in the bedsheet. Had he changed his mind, even slightly? "Whit," she said, "do you want me to have it?"

"We'll talk about that over the weekend."

"I'm not *asking* you. I'm planning to do it alone. You're carrying two—and that's no joke, that's real."

"We'll see." He lifted her onto the table. "Upsy-daisy."

Amo looked around, saw that the curtains were tightly closed.

Whit turned on the baby spots and washed his hands thoroughly, whistling the while.

"Those spots are killing my eyes."

"You ought to be used to that from modeling." He switched them off.

"No, Whit. They use strobes now that go on and off very fast."

"Here." He handed her an old necktie. "Put this over your eyes."

Amo lay there on the white sheet, feeling somehow like the sacrificial victim on the Aztec stone. Why did she think that?

"Slide forward now," said Webb. He took her skirt and turned it up so that only the sheet covered her. The turned-up skirt ballooned under her arms and over her chest like an umbrella turned inside out. She had to press it down to see.

"Now spread your legs apart with your feet out. Pretend these books are stirrups." He placed her feet wide apart on the *Random House Dictionary of the English Language* and the *World Book Encyclopedia*. Then he arranged the sheet so it covered her from waist to knee and she couldn't see beyond it.

Her knees rose before her like two quivery snow mountains. The most helpless position in life, thought Amo—for sex, for childbearing, and for the doctor was worst of all.

Whit turned on the spotlights, washed his hands once more, and put on rubber gloves. "Ready now, Amo?"

"Be careful, Whit. Don't hurt me. This means a lot to me." Hot lights and fear made her sweat. She forgot to put the necktie over her eyes.

"Why should I hurt you? Just lie very still. You may feel the instruments but don't move a muscle."

Whit inserted the speculum or spreader, that cold unnatural forcer. Once in awhile Amo saw his head with the tiny light like a third eye in the center of his forehead. The light cast striped war-paint shadows over his face, pale green and orange.

Amo felt an uncomfortable stretched sensation, even painful, as if the speculum were dilating her cervix. The pain was like menstrual cramps, only induced from outside. Why did he have to do that to examine her?

Through a mist of weakness, Amo lifted her head. "What are you doing?"

"Lie still," he commanded. "Don't move. It's dangerous."

The pain increased. Amo sweated but she didn't move. Then a torrent of horror went through her, head to toe, and she knew for sure what he was doing. Without moving a muscle, she said very distinctly, "Stop that, Whit. Stop trying to abort me."

With that, he plunged what felt like an ice pick into her and she screamed.

"Look what you made me do," said Whit.

Amo groaned and whimpered, contractions beginning, pain scraping raw through her beyond pain, appalling her entire body.

"Why did you jerk like that?" Whit snarled. "Now I'll have to finish it."

Blood came through the sheet. "Trying to kill me," Amo breathed, petrified.

"No, I can't. You might hemorrhage." Now Whit was sweating. Quickly he packed her bleeding parts with hard cotton and removed the speculum. "Get your coat!" he shouted, then remembered to help her to her feet.

Whit helped Amo to the car. Her feet didn't seem to want to move; they may as well have been made of rags. She rode slumped—conscious, semiconscious—as he raced across town to Roosevelt Emergency Clinic.

"Why not your own hospital?" asked Amo.

"Dangerous," was all he said.

Whit swerved into the Emergency Entrance and braked the car. Two ambulances were parked outside. No one was in sight. Whit helped Amo to the entrance door.

"Go on in," he said. "I've got to park. Tell them you're miscarrying."

Amo stood there wavering.

"Go on." He nudged her and scrambled back to the car.

Chapter 36
Hijack

Amo walked inside to the big reception room. Four or five people sat around—leg in cast, bandaged head. Amo saw the white nurse's uniform behind the desk, went up to it, and leaned. "Miscarrying," she said.

"Oh, my God." The nurse hollered to the two interns on duty.

They took one look at Amo and ordered a stretcher and an anaesthetist.

"Why did you do that to yourself?" said the tall pale one with glasses, Dr. Lawer.

"I didn't . . . Dr. Webb—parking the car."

The stretcher came. "Let's go," said the bald one with curly sideburns, Dr. Segal.

Amo glanced to the door. "Dr. Webb—?"

"No time, kiddo."

The attendants put Amo on the stretcher and off they went at a trot.

"Don't bounce," yelled Segal.

The nurse said, "No anaesthetist on duty. Pete's due."

"Where's Joe?" said Lawer. "Page him."

The nurse got on the intercom and paged both the man going off duty and the one coming on. Segal and Lawer followed the stretcher into the nearest operating room and began pacing, awaiting the anaesthetist who could watch the dials and the heartbeat. They placed Amo on the slab table, sheet draped over her stomach, lifted her legs, and placed her feet in the stirrups.

Both looked at her closely. "We can't wait," said Lawer, checking her pulse.

"No," said Segal. They both washed up quickly.

"Give her a local?"

"Nope. Too weak."

"Where's your sense of responsibility?" said Lawer, unpacking the cotton.

"Not . . . me," said Amo.

Segal shrugged. "Listen, kid, I don't know why you gouged yourself. But you got *our* work cut out for us. And you got to do your part."

"But I didn't. Dr. Webb—" gasped Amo but no one was listening.

"We can't wait." Lawer took over. He put his huge hands on her thighs. "We've got to do this without an anaesthetic. And you can't move a muscle—anywhere. Not even to scream. Dead still." He pressed hard on her thighs, pushing her knees outward.

Segal opened her with the speculum. "My God." He proceeded to do a D & C—a Dilation and Curettage, or Spreading and Scraping—without anaesthetic, which is rather like hara-kiri. Once gouged, the womb must be cleared of debris to prevent infection. Usually the woman lives if it's done by doctors, not hacks, under sterile conditions. The pain can be excessive if, like Amo, the woman has never had a child and is tight inside.

Without the cotton wadding, the horrible seething began again around the inner wound. Amo wondered about Whit only until the first cut from the ice-pick scissors, a jab to the core, trying to core the apple without tearing it apart.

"Stop, stop," she pleaded, not moving.

Segal stopped. "Your muscles are clenched. If you can loosen up, it won't hurt as much."

"But I—" Amo's head swung from side to side.

"Don't jerk," shouted Lawer, "not a move. You could hemorrhage."

"Wait! Can't I have painkiller?"

"Nope. Dangerous."

"Wait!" she spoke quickly before he could start again. "Please don't push my legs—it hurts. I'll be still."

Lawer looked doubtful but stayed to the side with his heavy hand on one knee and shoulder.

Amo gripped the edge of the slab table and Segal began working again. The ice pick turned into a knife that carved ragged meat from inside her and brought it out. Rusty knife, bloody meat. Pain so immense she thought her body would break in two.

"Stopstopstop," she said when she could stand it no longer.

The doctor stopped, sweating.

Amo endured the awful searing after the blade. "How long—?"

"About ten minutes—*if* you relax. If you can move down on the instruments, it won't hurt as much."

"I—how—?" said Amo.

"Wish we had some booze for you," said Lawer.

"Ready?" Segal began again the interior cutting and trimming.

Amo's head rolled from side to side and sweat salted her eyes. Her body grabbed the pain, got in its way, stopped it and felt it. If she could just remove her body, the pain would flow away without touching. She wondered how women in labor could scream; it would tear her apart. How did he expect her to push down on the pain? Didn't he know her body would quit?

"Stop!"

Segal stopped again. "Five minutes."

Lawer shook his head. "Poor crazy broad."

"Ready?" said Segal.

Amo nodded, gripped the edge of the table with hands that had turned to mush. Finally she forced her muscles to unclench and pushed down on the pain, accepting it, swallowed by it, for one ecstatic moment conqueror of the unconquerable, possessor of the external circumstance, the microcosm abdicating, diffusing, and thereby devouring the universe. Till the microcosm, small, could hold no more and collapsed on the slicing edge of the reeling universe of pain, clinging to murmuring eyes, overcast ears, fleeing pierced body, drowning in heat white and faceless till she slipped over the edge and lost consciousness.

This sixty-four-year-old Maruvian girl with her gray hair, sag and bag, sits alone on the cot, listening to the heat in the pipes, wondering what went wrong. She'd let them down. They'd let her down. Should she have the face-lift, the only way to face life again? Why did she turn forty and become sixty-four to all the men? She had the face-lift and everybody loved her again.

In her shimmering silver mini, she marched up the aisle of the Jumbo and rapped on the overhead rack for attention. "Ladies and gents, how'd you like to go to Maruvia?" she asked. The whole crowded plane cheered, first class and tourist, except for one creature in a wig who shrieked, "We're being hijacked!" Amo trilled with laughter, "Of course, you are." She held aloft a velvety pink object that was oblong with two folds. "This is my mini-accelerator, my all-purpose mini-control. Once I attach it anywhere in the cabin, we'll reach the speed of light and be on our way."

"Right on," shouted the passengers, "take it away, love!" All eager to depart the Solar System except for the pilot who appeared just as she attached the mini-control. Up/out/away they went at lightning speed and Amo's body—the waves, the flow, the tortion—relaxed as it had not been since her arrival on Earth.

As she floated on light speed, the passengers began to cough and choke. The plane was beyond the capacity of the oxygen equipment and slowly, smiling, reassuring her, the passengers choked, gasped, and died.

Amo had only one super-oxygenator mask, which she herself didn't really need. Should she give it to the remaining young woman, twenty-five, or the handsome pilot, thirty-five? Who should she save and take with her to Maruvia?

The pilot grabbed for the super-oxygenator mask. Amo gave him a shove and handed the mask to the gasping girl. The two of them had to fight him off. Finally he collapsed, died.

"I would've given it to him," said the dewy girl.

"I know," said Amo, "but he's killed me once too often."

"He doesn't mean it—it's his Drive."

"He *does* it."

As she and the girl she's saved head toward Maruvia, Amo realizes she's always been in love with the Wrist Radar. That voice, that mellow, soothing, admonishing accompaniment through life . . . she had to know him. Tumbling through space dreaming of love, love she'd never known yet always perceived, love that had left her exhausted but insatiable, like knowledge she never hoped to see and never ceased to imagine. Careening through space, eagerly she awaited her twenty-six-year-old lover as she died in her sleep, in the midst of life, in her dream of existence . . . trying to bore through infinity from sheer desire.

Back through gloggy wavy gray, setting into place the doctor's face which said, "It's all over." He pumped her full of penicillin and the nurse put her in a little room to rest.

Later the nurse waked her and mopped her face with a cloth and buttoned her clothes, since Amo's hands shook. Amo hobbled to the desk to fill out the report. She couldn't feel her legs or arms, only the vast aching crater in the center of her body.

"How're you feeling?" Segal came over.

"Okay, now." She sat down cautiously in the chair, handed over her Double Cross & Shield card.

"How did you start your abortion—miscarriage, whatever?" asked the nurse.

"I didn't," said Amo weakly. Talking exhausted her. "Dr. Webb—Whitney Webb—did. I thought he was just examining me."

"Oh God, not again," said Segal.

"Yes, again," said Amo woozily. She gave them his name and number and explained the relationship briefly.

The nurse dialed the number, exchanging glances with Segal. "Yes . . . yes. . . . Are you sure?" she said and hung up. "His answering service says he left at six o'clock this evening for Boston. He phoned just before he hopped on the Shuttle."

It wasn't accidental. He planned it. Amo sat, amazed.

Segal leaned down, confidential, "You shouldn't pull this crapola." He bonged his head. "They'll think you're out of your bird."

Amo probed his eyes, doubting she could get through to him. "Why would I? We knew enough doctors to arrange it in fifteen minutes."

Segal threw his arms in the air. "Who knows the

harebrained motives of frightened people—panic, hysteria, guilt."

Undoubtedly Whit's excuse, thought Amo.

"Just be glad you're alive, kid. Another five minutes and—kiiiiiik!" He ran his finger across his throat as if to slit it.

"Yes. Thanks," said Amo. "Really thanks." Survival was always tentative.

"Here, I'll take you home in the ambulance," said Segal, ignoring the scolding nurse and grabbing the keys.

Segal took Amo home in the ambulance for no better reason than that he was in the mood to drive a white ambulance with the red siren on.

"You live here?" said Segal, on reaching the D.O.D.

"Yes," said Amo. "Pity the poor lass."

"You listed—in the book?"

"Yes."

"Okay if I call?"

"You married?"

"No."

"Okay."

Segal helped her up the stairs.

Chapter 37
Sueño

Over the weekend Amo ached and wept, talked to W.R., and plotted revenge against Whit. The spongy red pain contracted and expanded with hatred while she slept.

Suspended in the air out her window over the garbage heap, Whitney Webb and Malachi Stein. All three sitting on night air. Why was Mal there?

Amo twirled, quick drew the fluted ray gun from the silver holster, tossed it in the air like a baton, and caught it. She aimed it at Whit and Mal, said, "Phoom phoom, die die," and put it back on her hip. Toying with them, hiding her rage.

Whitney scowled as you do at a child who's not being at all funny.

Malachi picked her up, lifting her high so the gun belt indented his chest with outlined bullets, and Amo's mound, like warm baked bread, heated the niche below his heart. "Man, you're turning me on."

"Let go!" Furious—his hard fingers burned like the blows he'd long since forgotten—Amo pushed her knees toward his groin and he let her down fast, looking hurt. Malachi the actor.

The bastards, thought Amo. Instant forgiveness is what they expect. No, total forgetfulness. After all, I'm a woman. Wipe it out. They have. Pulsing with pain, Amo assumed a Western stance, hand resting on holster. "Think I'll knock off the two of you since you happened by."

"You were always a fanatic," Whit pronounced, "a paranoid schizophrenic." Tanned hands folded under chin, blue inspection sat complacently in his stony face under that boyish all-American hair.

Amo sneered. "When are you going to stop sentimentalizing yourself and Nazi-fying other people?"

"Ha ha," Mal cackled, "the old shiv."

"Right," raged Amo, "right up inside of me. Whit, why did you abort me against my will? And Mal, why did you beat me up? I ended up in the hospital both times."

Both men sat with their heads down, as if zonked into silence. Challenged. Set back, but not for long. Whitney raised his head first. "How did I know you were going to jerk like that?" he brushed it off.

"Yes," said Malachi, "how did *I* know you were going to jerk like that?"

They looked at each other. "She can be very difficult," said Whit.

"You noticed," said Mal.

They smirked, arms crossed, establishing the bond.

At that moment Amo saw red splashes of blood

appear magically out of white faces and body shirts and palsy grins. Red splurts of fame that would—yes! yes, it was true!—would sell her book. Keep it selling for years, if she could do it. If she could kill. If she could be as casually lethal as they were.

If only she had the venom to do it—be a killer. At least in jail she'd be *with* people. Rest behind bars—no more striving, no more solitary. She could sell this story of ethical murder, a killing for the women of the world. Then unload *The Gobbling Deficiency*—the real book—as a spin-off. Opportunity had finally knocked for Amo. Dreams of glory from jail, from revenge. From anywhere would do.

The two men smiled comfortably at each other. Mal screwed his finger into his temple, "Amo's a bit flaky."

Whitney took on a tone, "It's clinical."

Gingerly she picked up the *banderilla*. She gored them both and was left teasing the night air, tossing on the bed, but she hadn't seen the blood. So she went back to sleep and saw Amo twirl, quick draw the fluted ray gun from the silver holster—better, much better—and aim it at Whit and Mal. "Phoom phoom, die die." She shot them with lasers. They bounced then blood appeared like fresh streams of vindication. Fresh flowing tears of Amo the dreamer. Flowing round Earth, tears and blood, from so many. Amo the dreamer. She came from a venerable line—the good and the unsung.

Chapter 38
Hip, Hip

On Monday Amo's literary agent phoned. "Where the hell have you been?" barked Amo's agent who never barked. "Didn't you get my Pfaff letter?"

"What?"

"That idiot you lived with said he forwarded it. What's wrong with him? I had a hell of a time getting this number—he acted like he didn't know you."

"Pfaff—what letter?"

"They wrote today and made us an offer." Curt laughed, "Getting itchy because they hadn't heard from us." He read the second Pfaff letter to Amo:

April 4, 196–

DEAR CURT:
Except for the office Gobblers, everybody here is very impressed with *The Gobbling Deficiency* by Amo Coove. I love it all —Maruvia with its UP (Universal Peace), the Time Stopping Pill, visibility diffusion, time and space diffusion, free transmission of Mind, Body and Feeling Hypes, integrated skin color, Transcendence, but probably most

of all the Interconsciousness System by which all Maruvians feel as much for others as for themselves, and which causes Amo so much terror here on Earth. We Earthwomen understand only too well the results of our own humanity and empathy—food for Gobblers.

Cogent—pungent—well constructed. Poly authorizes me to offer you $4,000 on signing, another $4,000 on publication. Phone today if possible.

Best,

BETSY CHENEY BOGDIKIAN,
Senior Editor
Pfaff & Company

Amo nearly went into shock. "You—you mean somebody wants to buy my novel?"

"It's high time they came to their senses," shouted Curt with hilarity. "At the bottom of the first letter, there's a note from Pfaff himself. Says, 'The most ingenious mythology I've read in years. Polycarp Pfaff, President.' Hey, how's that?"

"Hey, that's . . . unbelievable!"

There in the lordly Pfaff offices Poly Pfaff smiled at Amo. "You look like a model."

"I was," smiled Amo. She'd expected the scowling white-maned eminence who'd been lately replaced by his lanky auburn-haired son. "You look like a movie star."

In came Betsy Cheney Bogdikian, his wife, who greeted Amo as if she were a person, a person of capacity, even talent. Betsy looked the way Amo wanted to—pale and haunted, as if she were a veritable tuning fork of literary sensibility. "It's a thrill to read something original," said Betsy, eyes level and appreciative.

Amo was stunned.

Other editors and PR people came in to meet her and stood around the room, observing deferentially. Amo had never been treated so nicely. They acted as if they could see her. They treated her like she was a blooming genius. Pfaff put his feet up on his desk and his arms behind his head to stretch his lanky form and Betsy Bog, as she was called, perched on the windowsill and Amo swiveled in a kidney chair and they all toasted each other's perception and brilliance.

Amo hadn't been treated so well since the day years back when she posed as Tidbit of the Month. But Frick Pedlar expected a payoff. What did Pfaff want? A good book. A good book and incidentally, much later on with the galleys, Amo's body. She slept with him eventually because she wanted to, though she resented his power. She liked him because he never pushed it, and one night after going through minuscule editorial changes, it happened. Amo was well aware she could hurt the book if she said no. Better to mollify his ego and curiosity—as well as her own— and hope he'd then trot contritely back to Betsy. Which he did. Then they could all be friends.

The moment she got back to the D.O.D., Amo

phoned Mr. O'Donovan at Bellevue to tell him the good news. "I'm sorry," said the voice on the other end, "but he died last night."

Finally Amo phoned her Earthmother in Atlanta who sounded like a friendly judge pleased at her law clerk's progress, surprised, increasingly surprised, and at last, affectionate and interested.

"You haven't phoned in a year, Amo—since you moved in with Whit the guru," her mother admonished with Southern lilt.

"I knew what you wanted to hear, and I couldn't call till I had it to tell you."

"The book, you mean?"

"Of course, sweet Mommy. Hip, hip, hooray!"

"Suppose it was never bought. Would you ever have phoned?"

"Maybe not," said Amo. "What's the use of phoning to say you're going down the drain?"

"I care—and so does Sybil. And cut out that Mommy bit."

"How's Sybil?" They'd been together eight years now, the Judge and Sybil.

"Fine, dear."

"Ai ai ai ai aiiiiii!" shrieked Amo. "Do you suppose this is the happiest day of my life?"

"Probably, dear."

"Remember when I was a Tidbit in *Meat*, a mere morsel for the boys? Ha, ha! I've grown up."

"Gobble, gobble," said Mommy the Judge. "Careful, Amo."

Chapter 39
Instant Selfhood

Amo flew to her old haunts that she hadn't visited since she moved East with Whit, the guru. She flipped into the corner luncheonette where she'd been the star. Milt and Max, owners and fans, would point her out to customers as a famous model. Bud, the retarded delivery boy, could always tell her which pinup magazine she'd hit that month. Milt and Max didn't seem exactly stunned.

"Ya alweez said ya was writin' a great book, kid," said Max.

Amo was spilling over. "It's much *much* more important than modeling—you see that?" She jumped up and down, holding onto a luncheon stool.

"Nuttin's more important dan dat body," said Milt, and Bud blushed adoringly and everybody went ho ho ho.

Amo jabbed her arm into the air, posing as Joan of Arc whose chest stuck out. "On to the literary wars!" she piped, and danced down the street to the drugstore.

The drugstore gang used to convene irregularly

about cocktail hour when Cyclone finished sparring at the gym, Seymour finished writing his movie review, and Amo wound up a modeling job or Go-See. Cyclone, black and 6′6″, strummed background guitar while Amo and Seymour worked over the latest books, movies, plays. Amo peeked in and they were both there. She practically leapt at them with her news.

"No," Seymour kept saying, "no!"

"Yeh, mama, yeh," crooned Cyclone.

They nodded to each other, made a basket of their arms, and toted Amo down the street where they had a drink to celebrate.

Back home again she phoned Segal and Duane and Benno and Jay and Russ and Geller and Whit's mother, Simone. She wondered if Simone had something to do with it.

"No, my dear, I hadn't discussed it with anyone yet. But I'm intrigued with the book, and so pleased." After a pause Simone said, "I'm sorry you and Whitney broke up, Amo. I'm afraid the boy's not quite ready for someone like you."

Amo considered telling Simone about the abortion, but she let it go. Why hurt Simone just because Whit hurt her? Simone invited her to Sunday dinner and Amo said grand. Now that Whit wasn't between them, they could be friends.

Amo phoned Steve Luks who asked her out to celebrate. Furry gypsy Luks—she didn't yet know they'd be going together for the next year, to be followed/overlapped/interrupted/destroyed by the test pilot, the law student, the filmmaker, the political reporter, the young cop, the novelist (you can bet they told each other a lot—of nothing), the composer, the painter (who, like Everest, were simply there). Back to Jay the TV correspondent who was now divorced, then Nacho came to town from Mexico after his wife died in childbirth, then. . . . She had no idea how much she'd want Luks once she slept with his caring eyes, stumpy beaver body, rockhard dipstick, and vast humanity.

In the peasant French place, the Brittany, she told Steve about Whitney and the abortion. He seemed chilled but not as astounded as she had expected.

"Why, Steve? I didn't expect any help with the baby. Did he think I'd blackmail him afterward?"

"I doubt it." Steve mused, "I think he was punishing you for taking on the world like men do. For being out of line—"

"For the book?"

"For having the gall to write, and getting published. If no one had ever bought it, he'd have liked you better."

"He knows about it?"

"Sure," said Steve. "He told me about it yesterday."

"He must've read that first letter from Pfaff—that I never got. Yes," Amo recalled, "then he asked me over. Oh, Jesus."

Steve pressed her hands.

"Steve, can I sue him?"

"You won't get anywhere. He's covered." He squeezed her hands together. "You know how he met Chelo? She was his secretary—handled his office, *his* problems. That's what he likes. You were too much for him."

"But that's so—cowardly," Amo said with distaste.

"I'm not a coward," offered Steve, and proposed a toast to the book. Back at the D.O.D., Steve squeezed one hipped cheek with his ham hand and said, "I'll give you a week to get well."

Amo smiled, "Maybe two, Steve."

In ecstasy Amo called W.R. and relayed the good news.

AMO: "We pulled it off, W.R. At long last—love! They even like *The Gobbling Deficiency* title."

W.R.: "I'm proud of you, A.M.O. We all are. We await publication eagerly, and the effect on Earth's state of mind."

AMO: "Don't expect too much, W.R."

W.R.: "Sorry about the abortion, A.M.O., but I warned you about that Gobbler—"

AMO: "A Gobbler from the first nip—I should've known."

W.R.: "You're aware, though, that the baby was a substitute for the book?"

AMO (sighing): "In a sense, W.R. The book is what I always wanted most. But I wanted the child."

W.R.: "The Transcendence Network is even now broadcasting your success to the Interconsciousness System so that all may absorb and share it."

AMO: "W.R., I've told you the difference. Publication here is *not* automatic dissemination to the Earth mind. Don't get your hopes up." But she was too happy to listen to her own advice. "You know what recognition is—it's identity. Now I have myself—I'm a person—and I don't have to commit suicide."

W.R.: "Suicide?"

AMO: "That's what most people here do—commit suicide then linger on till death. Recognition is *everything* on Earth. It shouldn't be—it's too tenuous. There isn't enough to go around."

Amo had been slowly dying without self-esteem because for her, it depended not only on her work but its acceptance. Now, like a Mind, Body and Feeling Hype, she had been jabbed in the arm with instant selfhood. On Maruvia, everybody got one. Here, only a few. Almost no self-esteem permitted on Earth. There was some immense horror involved in the lethal demand for individual success. People turned into sharks competing for bits of soul food. The competition had become too ferocious for the fittest, unless that meant only the man-eaters.

She'd lucked out. Without Pfaff, she'd be another frustated compensating Lady Madonna trying to venerate her role for lack of something better to do. Or more likely, a hooker and porno film star. *Every*body was doing porn now; sex was In as never before. Because without recognition, Amo could not respect herself. Amo was very American.

From Tidbit to Househump, Amo had moved, from erotic sex symbol to domestic sex slave, from model to maid. Yet from beneath the rubble of her life, her

actual self—her work—had surfaced with her book.
The book quite literally saved her life. Would it take
it?

When Steve came by ten days later, Amo said, "The
foot's not pushing on my head, the chains fell away.
I'm floating—so lightly."

"You feeling pretty good?" Steve sat her on his
sturdy knees and kissed her. "Yes, you do."

Pseudo-love, Whit had said. "You know anything
about pseudo-love, Lucky?"

"What love isn't?" said Steve, rounding her breast
with his palm.

She rested her chin on his head as her nipple
blossomed. Love is need.

His face pleased her. She saw nimbleness, vibrancy,
soul. Everyone thirsted after love, thirsted to give it,
though nobody could keep it up for long.

Chapter 40
The Lit Tidbit

On Publication Day nothing happened.

Amo bought all the papers and scanned them for mention of *The Gobbling Deficiency*. Nothing. She looked outside. No banners in the sky. Nothing to link the day to Amo. For a week she'd been in a state of near paralysis from fear—fear that after all the work and rising expectations induced by publication, the book would be ignored. Like a penny dropped off the Empire State, a raindrop in the rain.

She began to tremble, shivering hot and cold. In rapid succession the next week, she was downed in a plane crash and eaten by sharks, was revisited by the old cancer which spread throughout her system, suffered tapeworm, the guillotine, and finally a heart attack which began with suffocation . . . choking . . . couldn't breathe.

Lucky phoned. "Have you seen the review?"

"What?" gasped Amo in the midst of the attack.

"Today's *Times*—it's good, though the reviewer has a reality hang-up."

"Yeah," Amo shouted, "yeah?" She recovered instantly and ran to the luncheonette for the *Times*.

Milt and Max had saved ten papers for her. "We was wonderin' when ya'd get here."

Amo read it, giggling at the good parts, glum when the reviewer didn't catch on (the bad parts). "He thinks I'm imaginary," she mused to no one in particular. She read:

> . . . Originality that will carry the reader beyond his farthest imaginative scope—a spaced-out mythology with a spellbinding cast of characters. The sort of book that women seldom do well, it causes one to speculate whether some thoroughly adept professional is spoofing us once again, this time with Barbarella up front. The jacket copy tells us "Miss Amo Coove" was once Tidbit of the Month in *Meat* magazine. And the cover shot proves it. Wowee, kids! Hat off to Miss Coove, whoever he/she may be.

In a fury Amo gathered up the various versions and rewrites of her novel, put them in the Mexican basket, went up to the *Times* unannounced, and slung them on the reviewer's desk. After the initial shock, he seemed quite friendly. He had meant it as a compliment, he said. Gobble, gobble. They had a drink.

The *Times* carried a story about it. The *Village Voice*, *Screw*, and the *Daily News* unearthed and published some nudes of Amo. *Cosmo* and *Esquire* did the same but *Meat* ignored her, she and Frick being *enemigos* still. Amo phoned Poly Pfaff to apologize but he was ecstatic.

"We're going ahead with the Lit Tidbit promo—the literary Tidbit. We'll all make a mint. At least, we'll up the paperback money."

"But I was hoping that phase was over," said Amo.

"You want your novel to sell or go down the drain?" boomed Poly.

"What does Betsy think?"

"The same as you do. But we've got to run with the tide before it goes out. How long you think we can interest the public in a book? Two weeks—a month if we're lucky." There was a strain to Poly's voice when he went hogwild PR. It wasn't natural to him.

"Let me speak to Betsy."

Betsy came on. "I'm here, Amo."

"What do you think of the Lit Tidbit?"

"Awful, insulting. But your book is important. We've got to float it somehow."

Poly got back on the line. "What do you say?"

"Gobble, gobble," said Amo. "Nobody will see what the book is *about*."

"Be grateful, Amo. This is ad money we didn't budget for you."

"Okay," said Amo sadly. "Do it your way."

Simone wrote a thoughtful review in the *New Yorker*, and W.R. wafted a glowing one to P.R. Out of town followed the *Times*, almost line by line in some cases. Amo appeared on several local TV shows and signed copies of her novel in several bookstores.

Then the billboard appeared on Times Square—a full nude of Amo, only slightly abstracted, with her legs open and the title, *The Gobbling Deficiency,* drooling out in art nouveau.

Poly and Amo and Lucky went to see it. Amo fainted dead away. Fortunately Poly had alerted the Press who shot Amo stretched out on the pavement under her giant fleshtan replica. National TV news carried it and all the papers except the *Times.* The *Daily News* covered its front page with the shot under the banner, NUDE DWARFS NUDE. The *Post* had fun: LIT TIDBIT IN SNIT.

Amo called the *Times* to thank them for not running it. Then they ran it. People were terribly shocked, horrified. They rushed to the bookstores in unprecedented droves.

Amo became the Lit Tidbit. She was interviewed on TV by Ron Larceny on the No. 1 Night Show. The whistles began as Amo appeared in a silver miniskirt with molten top and sparkling silver pantihose. Her silver space shoes looked like the wings of a bird with the body as platform. Even when she was still, the glitter seemed to wiggle.

"Why?" said Larceny. "Why?"

"That's a retouched shot," Amo explained. "They got rid of the bikini and inserted the title instead. I refer to it as a media massage."

Larceny tugged at his choirboy collar, rolled his cheery berry eyes. "Why don't we escalate from Times Square to Maruvia?"

"Happily."

"How did the Maruvians hit on the notion of integrated skin color?"

"We computed average skin color and dosed fetuses

with the necessary melanin to solve our race problems aeons ago. Now, of course, our genes produce it."

"No offense,"—Larceny grinned at the black comedian who'd preceded Amo—"but you look lily white to me."

"That's an Earthly effect, like the blonde hair and the shape." Amo recrossed her silvery legs. "A bit corny, I know."

That broke up the audience nicely.

"What can you demonstrate?" Larceny asked. "Can you show us poor Earthlings any of these Maruvian advances?" He winked broadly at the audience.

"I can demonstrate a simple visibility diffusion." Amo jumped up, all silver sparkle, and said to the audience, "I will spin around and you'll notice that when I'm directly sideways to your eye, my form will disappear."

The audience shifted about.

"Ahem," went Larceny, brow arched in simulated interest.

The band produced a barrel roll.

Amo spun around and her silver skirt swirled up and the top of those thighs peeked at the world and that silver mound rounded by. Various people, including Larceny, blinked and shook their heads but the audience burst into tumultuous applause.

"Invisible at the center! Disappeared for *that* long," came the cries. "Like a prism!" someone said. "Optical illusion," said another, "she may not be there at all."

Ooooohs and aaaaahs from all sides.

"You see?" said Amo.

Ron Larceny went to scratch his head but stroked

his sideburn instead. "Um—yeah," he said archly, coy as a gingersnap. The black comedian rolled his eyes on cue.

Larceny began referring to the book as *The Gabbing Proficiency* and wanted to know why women gossip so much. Amo explained about the Gobblers and he asked why she was so eager to castrate men. Amo said she wanted to stop the castration of women. "Oh yeah, an eye for an eye, like savages," said he. "How 'bout a bust in the mouth instead?" The audience roared.

That night, Lucky beside her, Amo watched herself on the No. 1 Night Show, performing like a trained silver seal, glistening, mobile, cute cute cute. She whirled, she twittered. The audience loved her general cutie-tootness.

Amo threw up. The horror was she was self-trained. *She* had put the façade up front, responding to demand. A public body, a female impersonator. A public body that had nothing to do with Amo inside—no similarity. A simulation of her desire to please combined with, of all misfits, her anxiety for literary recognition. Amo heaved her disgust into the bowl, waving Lucky away from the bathroom door.

"But Amo," said Lucky, "you were adorable. That's the name of the game."

Amo threw up. Nobody found out what *The Gobbling Deficiency* was about. They didn't even get the title right, once the yuks began. Nobody listened. Nobody insisted that they *hear*, least of all Amo. Amo had remained invisible and adorable, as always—a real Lit Tidbit.

"You were grand," Poly phoned. "It was really fun."

"Put Betsy on."

"Some performance, Amo." Betsy's voice sounded strange.

"But stupid," said the invisible woman.

Poly grabbed the line. "You're booked on the No. 2 Night Show. How about a little more chest, eh?"

"Sheer class, Poly," said Amo, chained again.

"Ignore him, Amo," said Betsy. "You do it your way."

"Thanks, Betsy. This time I will."

Lucky folded her in his bearish embrace. "You can't change the world, Amo. Everybody's tried."

The No. 2 Night Show, the *Rich Savvy Show*, booked Amo because of her success on the competition and, of course, the book. She arrived in the same silver mini and space shoes, to the purring approval of staff and cast. Like all novelists and minor characters, Amo was set to go on last. Finally she had the dressing room to herself.

Five minutes before she was due onstage. Amo changed into a pink T-shirt, jeans, and tennies. She wiped off the makeup, removed the fall added to her long mop of hair, and marched onstage.

Savvy looked up and Amo walked in a foot below the level of his gaze. "It's the little prop girl," said Savvy.

"It's me—Amo Coove. You just fanfared me in."

He half rose, blond and pink and not so big himself. "Where's your glitter?"

"I want to tell the folks about my book, *The*

Gobbling Deficiency." Arms crossed, Amo stood there rocking in her tennies. Savvy looked as if he might yell *"Cut"* and chase her off so Amo sat down cross-legged at the footlights and signaled for a mike.

"Okay, okay," he shrugged, lifted his arms for audience reaction, and they clapped cheerfully. How often did they see a kid playing kick-the-can?

Amo jumped up and sat down next to Rich Savvy, smiling amiably. She could turn on a dime in those tennies.

Savvy laced his fingers. "Just in from the softball mound?"

"The merry-go-round," said Amo. "The music is grand but the trip's a downer."

"Quid pro quip," said Savvy, voice high with a drawling edge of cynicism.

Likable enough, thought Amo, resisting the urge to put her feet up on the low table in front of them.

"What's your pitch, kid?" Savvy held up the book. "What's *The Gobbling Deficiency?"*

"The male tendency to gobble up people—to put power before humanity, to rape the Earth. To kill ruthlessly, as long as it's for power, and give no quarter to goodness. To despise gentleness and be bored with sensitivity. To act like sharks."

"Yes, I see what you mean." He was small and once gentle; maybe he did. "Though that's quite a mouthful."

"Haw, haw." The audience got that one.

"On Maruvia," Amo went on, "we have the Interconsciousness System by which everyone feels for others as much as they feel for themselves. We can't hurt other people without feeling immense pain. We don't feel separated from others—or from ourselves. Earthwomen have this power. Earthmen do when children but they repress it."

Savvy chuckled with incredulity. "Why would anyone repress something as handy as that? You could wiretap the world and make a fortune."

The audience laughed gaily.

Amo tucked a foot under her to sit higher. "In order to *win,* you have to short-circuit your empathy." She put the other foot up till she was kneeling in the chair, leaning forward. "Masculinity today simply means Victory—over other men in success and power, and over women in sex and control." She sat back down in her chair. "If winning is everything, the end justifies murder. Yes, Earthmen would probably use the Interconsciousness System for wiretapping," she said sadly, slumping.

The audience was totally silent.

"That's the Gobbling Deficiency," she added, tears forming in her eyes.

Several women in the audience sensed it and great sobs were heard here and there.

"Have you ever been attacked?" said Amo. "I have. Not by dogs, by human males. In Boston men rape girl hitchhikers. Yesterday in New York a man threw two women out a hotel window. Vietnam, the Middle East, there's always a war. If war solves nothing, why do men keep fighting? Because secretly they don't *respect* anyone who's not a killer. If this were Maruvia, we could treat them, cure them." Amo reached to the audience with all the Interconsciousness at her command. "I'm afraid we have to fight them. Peaceably."

"Fight them," echoed several women loudly. "Peaceably."

"Push the foot off our heads." Amo stood up. "Invent the magic to unchain ourselves." She walked to the footlights. "Down with Gobblers! No more Tidbits for the boys!"

Many women were on the edge of their seats, eyes bright. The men looked at them, confused.

"Down with Gobblers!" Amo shouted, thrusting both arms into the air, looking every bit the Maruvian crime fighter.

Slowly about twenty women in the audience rose and joined the shout. "Down with Gobblers," they hollered, to everyone's amazement, before the cameras turned away. More women rose, shouted, stood on the seats.

"*Cut, cut,*" yelled Savvy and the bandleader. Various technicians ran on stage.

Cameras off, Savvy marched to Amo, smirking, looking helplessly comic—"That'll do, kid"—and tried to tug her offstage.

In an undertone, "I'll pull your hairpiece," Amo said with gleeful menace, and he let go.

Somebody pushed Savvy; he was small and stumbled.

Big shoulders lumbered toward Amo. One pinned her arms. She came down hard on his instep, he yowled and let go. The director.

From somewhere in the distant past, she hooked his leg, hauled his arms, and threw him over her shoulder.

As much as she hated to do it. Amo's strength was rage.

It was very still. High noon with strange weapons. Technicians with arms akimbo. Savvy, shaken, straightening his tie. Audience rumbling. Two security men slowly advanced. Hulking forms surrounding her, as in the primal night.

"Don't touch me," Amo shouted. "We'll riot!"

"Yeeaaaa, right on!" the women clamored, beating the chairs, stomping, clapping.

The advance stopped, halted in place, awaiting another signal.

"You see," said Amo, "the Gobbler in action. I say they're violent and they want to kill me for it."

"Okay, folks," Savvy grabbed a reassuring mike, "settle down now." He asked Amo calmly, "What on Earth do you women want?"

"Power. Pow—pow—power." The verbal bursts shot from the audience.

"Let's have a meeting," Amo hollered to the women. "Let's meet tomorrow."

"Central Park Skating Rink," someone yelled.

"Twelve noon," said another.

"Pow—pow. Down with Gobblers," they chanted. Amo waved and danced. "Pow—pow. Down with Gobblers!"

Amo ran to the edge of the stage with a side leap and click for joy, and jumped over the footlights into the audience.

The women met the next day. It was a beginning.

Chapter 41
G.M.C.Rerun

The women began to hold Anti-Gobbler meetings.
Amo spoke about the Maruvian Solution. Amo took
Betsy Bog to the giant Gobbler Gab where sixty
women discussed cures for the Gobbling Deficiency.
Amo began to make women friends. So did Betsy.
They discovered there were already groups, that they'd
never heard of, that had never heard of the book. But
Interconsciousness was in the air, like blue sky
breaking through pollution, hope after rain. Amo was
not an initiator but a joint inventor, as so often
happens.

Once more the Great Minor Celebrity appeared and
Amo suffered instant fleeting fame. What with
murder, mayhem, war, fraud, and the ongoing attempt
by the Gobblers to eat the world, public attention
wandered. Jabbed daily by the media and the
muggers, both industrial and private, folks forgot Amo
and her book in a month.

The trade—bookstores, local TV, paperback sales,
and movie moguls—remembered for three or four
months. *The Gobbling Deficiency* sold to paperback

for a decent sum, reported in the news as four times as
high. The problem with movie rights was that (male)
money directors and producers were fascinated,
almost sold, wanted to turn the Gobblers into women.
One powerful director swore he would not, that he'd
indicate why Gobblers happened, why women deserved, asked for, Gobblers, and how women had in
fact probably created Gobblers in the first place.
Things like that, like the victim being to blame. Amo
practically gave it away to a poor but respected woman
director.

Solvent for the first time on Earth, Amo managed to
get an apartment in the Village with two separate
rooms—a living room and a bedroom. At last she'd be
able to leave the D.O.D. Bidding good-bye to Milt and
Max, the drugstore gang, the memory of Mr. O'Donovan, and the crumbling familiarity, she almost sobbed.

The night before she moved, the D.O.D. caught fire.
The trashy court behind the building responded to a
cigarette tossed from a window and the flames caught.
Amo smelled something burning but she so often
breathed lethal fumes that she paid scant attention.

Firemen with axes stomped up the stairs, knocking
on doors and shouting, "Fire! Everybody out. Fire!"

Amo performed her Fire Drill quickly. She tossed
her writing in the Mexican basket and leaped down the
stairs, coughing. With the other tenants in old robes
and skimpy slippers, Amo stood outside on the filthy
pavement. Under the streetlight, she checked the
basket to be sure she had all of the new novel, plus
notes, begun in Whit's basement. All there—she

relaxed and smiled, coughing from the smoke. The fire went up the back, burning the garbage pile and Amo's window with the bars on it. She spent the night with Lucky.

In her Village apartment, Amo could sit in one room and know she had another, then stand in the other and see the one she'd left. Amo had never had more than one room. The living room faced a park wedge with tough, stunted trees. The bedroom faced a garden. Of course the garden was not hers. But she could see green.

Elated, Amo called W.R.

AMO: "We're beginning to hook up the Interconsciousness System, W.R. Here on Earth—at last."

W.R. (excited): "Then you can come back to Maruvia, my dear A.M.O."

Amo felt she was outgrowing W.R. But how could she dispose of her one perfect projection?

She stood at her new window, smiling stubbornly. In the park the dwarf trees pushed limbs into the city air. Like Amo.

By now Amo hoped she'd accreted enough identity to live alone in the midst of life. She was well into the new novel which lay scattered about her altar desk in a friendly and threatening fashion.

Amo sashayed outside to explore her new neighborhood. The blacks swirled through the park, hustling everything in sight. The old ladies sat their cold limbs on sunny benches, ignoring the panhandling bums staggering about. Couples leaned together. Newlymets chatted politely. Faggots waved their bottoms at passing jocks. Schoolchildren skated on the awful pavement, dogs paraded, pigeons pecked. Everybody bought the paper, went to the bank, missed the litter basket.

"Gobble, gobble," said a passing young woman to a surprised young man.

Amo laughed out loud. Home is home.

www.ingramcontent.com/pod-product-compliance
Lightning Source LLC
Chambersburg PA
CBHW061606170626
46811CB00001B/332